A
Harlequin
Romance

OTHER
Harlequin Romances
by JOYCE DINGWELL

Many of these titles are available at your local bookseller,
or through the Harlequin Reader Service.

For a free catalogue listing all available Harlequin Romances,
send your name and address to:

HARLEQUIN READER SERVICE,
M.P.O. Box 707, Niagara Falls, N.Y. 14302
Canadian address: Stratford, Ontario, Canada.

or use order coupon at back of book.

RED GINGER BLOSSOM

by

JOYCE DINGWELL

HARLEQUIN BOOKS   TORONTO
WINNIPEG

Original hard cover edition published in 1972
by Mills & Boon Limited, 17 - 19 Foley Street,
London W1A 1DR, England

© Joyce Dingwell 1972

SBN 373-01633-6

Harlequin edition published November 1972

Printed in Canada

CHAPTER ONE

'... TO my niece, Rowan Redland, a young woman I have never met, but if she differs from my other nieces and nephews who have been waiting for this for a long time she should be a much better choice, I give, devise and bequeath ...'

'Tch-tch.' Mr. Purkiss stopped short, looked annoyed with himself and with the document in his hand, then hastened to explain to the girl sitting on the opposite side of the desk: 'Your late uncle, Miss Redland, obviously did not employ an authorized person to draw up his will.'

'You mean,' inserted Rowan unhappily, for she was quite looking forward to being an heiress, 'it won't count?'

'By that do you imply that it is invalid?' frowned Mr. Purkiss. 'No, it is entirely acceptable. I was just deploring the wording, Miss Redland. Perhaps' ... polishing his glasses ... 'I can give it to you in proper legal phrasing.'

'Oh,' regretted Rowan, who was rather enjoying the detours, and wanted to hear more about her deplorable cousins.

'... to my niece, Rowan Redland,' resumed Mr. Purkiss, and he paused to nod confirmingly at Rowan, 'I give, devise and bequeath the whole of my estate both real and personal, but only if she carries on the said estate in the manner in which it is now being transacted, that is profitably as well as beneficially to those it serves, the judge of this to be my trustee Jonathan Saxby, and failing his complete satisfaction the estate then to be divided between—' Mr. Purkiss paused to say, 'There now follows a list of names.'

'Loris, Jessica, Gladwyn, Hal and Pearce,' recited Rowan knowledgeably. She added, 'Different surnames.'

'Is that so?' remarked Mr. Purkiss.

'Yes, there were six girls in Mother's family but only one boy, and the boy never married. The girls, like my mother, had only one chick apiece.' At Mr. Purkiss's rather bemused look, for the copy of the will had been flown from Australia, and he had gathered that Miss Redland's family had long since lost touch with their Colonial relations, Rowan explained: 'My mother recorded their names as babies in her Bible.'

'Hurumph,' nodded Mr. Purkiss. 'Well, there you are, Miss Redland. You have inherited your uncle's estate, but only, as you just heard, for so long as you conform to what this trustee, this Jonathan Saxby, deems satisfactory.'

'Hurumph,' said Rowan in her turn. Perhaps a sheep station, she was thinking forlornly; how on earth could I run that to satisfaction? Or a banana plantation – why, I don't even know whether the hands of bananas . . . it is hands, isn't it? . . . hang up or down. A vineyard . . . A—

'It's a refreshment room,' announced Mr. Purkiss, going through some papers. 'It's situated in the state of Queensland in a place called Cosy Corner. It's named Tom Thumb.'

'Oh,' beamed Rowan. She repeated joyfully, '*Oh!*' For a refreshment room she could run, especially one in a comfortable-sounding place like Cosy Corner and bearing the reassuring name of Tom Thumb.

Why, she could see it already. Strategically situated to snare the peckish passers, probably seating a modest but profitable twenty to thirty, paper napkins in a tumbler (she would change that to brightly checked cotton) and a light manageable menu offering dainty sandwiches and

6

cinnamon toast. For the more robust eater, she went further, perhaps welsh rarebit or scrambled eggs.

'Oh!' she breathed rapturously again.

'You mean you are actually interested, Miss Redland?' asked Mr. Purkiss, surprised. It seemed impossible to him that anyone could be elated by such a modest inheritance, especially with such a confining clause as 'carried on in the manner in which it is now being transacted.' Particularly, he thought, when the inheritance was so far away.

But — 'Oh, yes,' glowed Rowan. 'In fact I dream of something like this every lunch hour from one to two.'

'Indeed?' rather disbelieved the solicitor, who had dignified dinners personally delivered to his office from an exclusive restaurant each business noon, and who had no idea of what Rowan went through, since in the particular city sector where she worked there was only one over-crowded cafeteria, and since she had to eat there because Miss Grimbell's Select Hostel for Selected Young Ladies, of which she was one of the selected young ladies, did not provide packed lunch.

How often in the long queue had Rowan yearned for a tea-room of her own. All the girls had. They had even chosen the café curtains, the pattern of the china. The menu had been argued out, then agreed on, over a hundred times, and it was what she had just planned now, with, perhaps, scones and cream or layer cake as extras, though if Jonathan Saxby did not want extras, she would conform, yet ... confidently ... with a name like Tom Thumb in a place called Cosy Corner she had no fears.

She sat gloriously still and saw it all. Dainty white cups with a green elf with a feather in his peaked cap prettily imprinted on the china, the same folksy insignia on the apple-green pinafores of the two fresh young girls she would have to help her out. Perhaps a touch of music in the air, pleasant un-mod themes suitable for the not-too-young, Viennese waltzes, Two Little Girls in Blue. A 'Special' every day, like Aunt Jenny's Melting Moments, or—

'Miss Redland, I've spoken to you twice.'

'I'm sorry, Mr. Purkiss.'

'I am then to accept this on your behalf?'

'Oh, yes, please.'

'You realize you must leave almost at once? If you didn't, this trustee could consider you were not fulfilling your side to his satisfaction.'

'As it happens,' rejoiced Rowan, 'I had saved for a trip abroad and have my fare ready. I've had all the precautionary immunizations that Australia should require.'

'No ties, Miss Redland?'

'None at all. My mother was Australian and the only one of her family to leave Australia.'

'I see.' Mr. Purkiss closed up the will. 'Then all that is left for me is to shake your hand and wish you the best in Tom Thumb.' He rose and did so. 'At least,' he added, for he was a responsible person and had a daughter of his own around Rowan's twenty-odd years, 'you should be quite safe in a place called Cosy Corner and with a refreshment room called Tom Thumb.'

'Absolutely safe, Mr. Purkiss. Thank you, Mr. Purkiss. If you're ever in Queensland, Mr. Purkiss, do call in for scones and cream. Or cucumber sandwiches. Or—'

... Rowan was still adding to her menu (Tom Thumb inscribed on the top of it) as she closed the legal door.

Everyone at Miss Grimbell's Select Hostel for Selected Young Ladies, except Miss Grimbell who immediately mentally filled the coming vacancy, adding a little more board, drooled over Rowan's remarkable news.

8

'You could expand,' planned Miss Silver. 'There could be Tom Thumb tea rooms all over Australia.'

'So long as I have this one,' rejoiced Rowan, 'and I have, and I intend to hold it. Why, I'll do anything to appease this old trustee of my uncle's estate.'

'Caraway seed cake,' advised Miss Jones, 'the old people dote on it. Add it to the menu if it's not already on.'

'Possibly no teeth,' warned Miss Wyatt, 'and those seeds, so it could be worrying. No, best to keep to plain Madeira, Rowan.'

'My grandpa,' said Alice West, 'likes Chelsea buns.'

One of the girls found a map of Australia, and they all searched Queensland for Cosy Corner. They couldn't find it, but they found reassuringly English-y names like St. George, Inglewood, Withersfield (ignoring Nugga Nugga, Cungelella), so all was well.

Within a week a letter arrived from Jonathan Saxby. He wrote a fine firm hand for an old man.

He went straight to the point, no 'dear', no 'I have received a communication from Mr. Purkiss.'

'Not even,' regretted Alice, peering over Rowan's shoulder, 'a "hoping this finds you well as it leaves me at present." At least I expected that.'

But the dear old man had wisely considered directing Rowan as more important. 'Change plane at Sydney, N.S.W., for plane to Brisbane, Queensland, change plane at Brisbane for plane to—' There followed another of those reassuring respectable English names. Then: 'Pick up bus for C.C. and ask for T.T.' There followed 'Jonathan Saxby' in virile writing. What a wonderful senior citizen, Rowan raved.

She left London Airport, a fortnight later, everyone, except Miss Grimbell who was settling in the new boarder at a little more, there to see her off.

9

Rome, Karachi, New Delhi, Bangkok, Singapore, Darwin . . . they went excitedly past.

Then Rowan was landing at Kingsford Smith, Sydney, but not looking at Sydney beyond the airport because the Brisbane plane was ready to take off at once. It was the same at Brisbane, the smaller craft that served that respectable name from which she was to bus it to C.C. and T.T. was due to leave immediately.

This last aerial hop took much longer than Rowan had anticipated, and for the first time she realized the between-places-spaces of this down under scene. Looking at the map in London it had only been an inch or so. Now it was miles. Hundreds and hundreds of miles.

But at last they were there, and putting down in a field of paddy-weed and thistle . . . and very little else.

But a bus was waiting, and the driver said that yes, he went through C.C. Most of his pick-up, he told Rowan, was after C.C., but he was obliged to call at the airfield because it was down in the timetable. She would probably be the only passenger till C.C. He said, 'Hop in.'

Somehow it did not look a bus to take you to a busy metropolis, or even a thriving suburb. It had a distinctly battered look. All the windows were either cracked or broken, and Rowan soon knew why. There was only a narrow strip of bitumen, and if you didn't slow up and get to the side of it when oncoming traffic reached you, you copped it. That was what the driver said. 'I copped it,' he mourned.

He asked Rowan where in C.C. and she said, 'T.T.'

'Oh, yes, Tom Thumb.' – Thank heaven at least for that.

They were going through sugar country, and at any other time Rowan would have delighted in it, called out in pleasure at the patchworks of fields of cane in different stages and colours of growth making a vivid mosaic, but not now. She was growing uneasy.

Forests of spotted gum enfolded them next, then out again to pineapple plantations, then, where some hills rose up, banana slopes with flying foxes to collect the yellow loot. After that pawpaws. Macadamia nuts. More cane. Finally another crop that she did not know, but did not dare to ask the driver, because traffic was approaching, and he was edging to the verge to safeguard what glass he had left. But she looked at the sturdy green stalks with their rosy shoots and would have liked to have known what else besides sugar, timber, pineapples, bananas, pawpaws and nuts this remarkable state could grow.

All very nice, she applauded silently, but where ... *where* was any town?

She sensibly reminded herself that moderately close to London ... also, someone had once told her, tolerably close to New York ... you found space. But such space as this?

'C.C. coming up!' called the driver, and Rowan peered out. She saw nothing, no straggling outskirts promising something better closer in, she saw only the narrow bitumen and a line of haulage trucks tearing up that bitumen even more than it was torn up now. She turned and looked behind her and saw a procession of trucks there as well.

'Busy road,' she observed.

'It's a road between two points,' said the driver, 'and things have to get up and down. And glad I'd say that T.T. is about that. Tucker, I mean, miss. These hauliers have to be fed. They tell me there's to be an opposition. It generally happens when there's a good thing offering. Well, the truckies will soon sort that out. They know where the bread is buttered.' He laughed at his own pun. 'Here's Thommo's now.'

'Thommo's?' asked Rowan faintly.

'T.T.,' the driver reminded her.

'But,' said Rowan hollowly, looking at an ugly galvanized iron building adorned with a large notice bearing one huge word 'EATS', 'I'm wanting Tom Thumb.'

'Same place.' The driver began putting down her bags. He jerked his head to the name of the proprietor, as required by law, and Rowan read some small lettering ... and remembered.

Remembered. REMEMBERED.

'I always hated my surname,' her mother had said, 'because everyone laughed at Selina Thumb.'

Thumb. *Thumb!* Mary, Olga, Agnes, Dora, Frances, Selina and – and Thomas. Thomas Thumb. Uncle Thomas. Tom Thumb.

'Oh, no!' Rowan cried to herself.

'If you're still around C.C. and T.T. I'll b'seeing you, miss,' the driver was saying. 'I always eat where the truckies eat,' he went on, 'and so far they eat here. They're good customers for good grub, so it's no wonder that Thommo's, getting the crowd they do, are having opposition at last.' He looked at her curiously. 'You are stopping, miss?'

'Well,' said Rowan, 'I haven't come all this way for scones and cream.' She was dangerously near tears.

'Wouldn't get any,' grinned the driver. 'Just ring that bell.' He roared the engine and the bus moved off.

A truck pulled in where the bus had stood. Another truck behind it. The two drivers with their offsiders got off, looked Rowan appreciatively up and down, then pulled the bell which was of the ancient cow variety.

'Steak and eggs or eggs and steak?' called a voice somewhere in the galvanized horror. 'How many?'

'Four ... five if the lady is eating.'

'No,' said Rowan hurriedly, 'I mean a sandwich will do.'

'Four s. and e.'s coming up. One sandwich.' A man emerged practically at once from somewhere in the rear of the galvanized horror and slapped down four gargantuan plates of the biggest steaks Rowan had ever seen, each plate with three eggs apiece, on to an uncovered trestle table. Then bread and butter, a Tower of Pisa each of thick bread and butter. Tomato sauce.

'The lady's sandwich,' said the waiter next . . . a waiter, in battered jeans, black singlet and a hat at the back of his head? . . . and he thumped down a tower that rose even higher than the other towers. Each sandwich was a doorstop and there were at least ten of them.

'Corned dog and mustard pickle jake with you?' he asked as he went out again.

Tea came in the one pot, but the pot was almost an urn. The steak-eaters asked Rowan to pour. It flowed out dark and full of leaves but very hot. They all scooped sugar into it, dirty grey sugar. 'Unrefined from the crushing,' they grinned at her grimace, 'best sugar in the world, miss. Full of sun.'

She hardly had time to answer them before they had finished and were calling for the bill. They argued fiercely which one was to have the honour to pay for the sandwiches.

'But you mustn't,' protested Rowan, 'I mean—'

'Not every haul a lady pours,' they appreciated, and they all drew out notes.

It was beyond the calculations of the waiter, who called into the kitchen . . . Rowan supposed it was a kitchen . . . for help to sort it out.

It took a while for the cook to emerge, and when he did he was a complete surprise. He wore an immaculate white short-sleeved shirt and grey slacks and he took a pencil from the black sideburn at his ear.

'Now who is standing the sandwiches?' he said.

13

'No one.' Rowan stepped forward.

'Then that will be fifty cents, miss.'

The men argued again, but finally agreed to pay only for themselves, and departed with a friendly wave.

'Fifty cents,' said the man, putting the pencil back on his ear where it hid itself in the thick sideburn again.

'I—' began Rowan nervously, then she took a deep breath. 'I don't pay,' she informed him.

'You what?'

'I don't pay.'

'I thought that's what you said.' He waited ... and waited. 'Fifty cents, miss.'

'I suppose I could give it to you, but it would be silly.'

'Try me out and see if I laugh.'

'This has gone far enough.' Rowan was angry now. 'And so,' she added bitterly, 'has this wretched place. Tom Thumb, indeed!'

'Well, that was his name. Thomas Thumb.'

'Oh, I know. I mean I know *now*. I mean that had I known ... And to think' ... pitifully ... 'I've spent all I have getting here!'

'Getting ... You – you wouldn't be her, would you? You wouldn't be—'

'If you mean Miss Redland—'

'I do.'

'Then yes. And I didn't think I was coming to this galvanized horror. There was to be little café curtains, and girls in aprons, and a menu with sandwiches, and—'

'You just had sandwiches, didn't you?'

'Mine were wafer-thin ones. Cucumber. A bill of fare with scones and cream and cinnamon toast.'

'Wrong place, miss. Also' ... a scornful glance ... 'wrong girl. I warned old Tom about that, but would he listen? No. So long as you're here to keep her in line, Jon,

14

he said—'

'Jon? Not Jon—'

'If you mean Jonathan Saxby—'

'I do.'

'Then yes.'

'But you're not old. I mean not caraway seed old, I mean not Chelsea bun.'

'Miss Redland, are you well?'

'No, I'm sick.' Rowan sat down and poured herself more tea from the urn. Fishing out the leaves, she drank. It was vile. She added grey sugar and actually felt a little better. It must be that sun they crushed into it, she thought abstractedly. But the feeling of being better only lasted until the man put his hand in his pocket and took out an envelope and gave it to her.

'Cable,' he said laconically. 'Came before you came. It's for you.' He watched her open it.

It was from the loyal Grimbell girls, still thinking about her and about Tom Thumb. They had all recorded their names to the wire, so they must have shared the cost. The cable ordered blithely: 'Cinnamon toast for seven.'

It was then that Rowan wept.

Absorbed with her tears, she was not aware that he had prompted her up and propelled her out until she was there. There was the kitchen, and it was even worse. Certainly the table was not on trestles, but it was big and bare and chopped about, probably chopped from those unspeakable steaks. There was a bête noir of a range that took one entire side of the galley, and on the other side an outsized old-fashioned dresser crammed with the thickest china she could imagine. She felt quite sure if she had taken one of the plates out to the bitumen and dropped it, it would have stared back at her. Intact.

The range was red-hot, and since this was a latitude

where winter was only something heard of down south, or so the bus driver had told her, it was warm, to say the least.

She must have gasped so, for Jonathan Saxby, no doubt a native, looked proud of his un-cold part of the country and pointed out, 'Yes, we enjoy a steady seventy-five to eighty. That's why we're Cosy Corner.'

'But the fire . . .' she began.

'Thommo . . . your Uncle Tom always kept it glowing. He never knew when a truckie was pulling in, and truckies, as you may have noticed just now, don't wait.'

'Is that why you offered them only steak?'

'No,' he said.

'Then—'

'It's all,' he grinned, 'they order.'

'But breakfast, for instance. That is if you're open for breakfast.'

'Always open.'

'Then?'

'Steak.'

'Afternoon tea?'

'That would be late dinner.' He waited. 'Steak.'

'*I* was served sandwiches.'

'Which I see you left.'

'I didn't. I just didn't eat the ten of them.'

'We also,' he explained, 'sell a cut lunch for truckies on the run. That's why your sandwiches didn't take long.'

'On the run?' She decided to drop the sandwich subject.

'Trying to make wherever they have to make by a certain time. So it's corned dog and mustard pickle, black tea and pep pills.'

'What?' she gasped.

'Look, Miss Redland, we don't sell them the pills, we frown on them, but we're aware of them, and that's why we make the sandwiches thick and hot and the tea or coffee strong. We feel at least we help when we do that.'

'But why? Why do they do it? I mean the keep-awake things?'

'Ambition for their families,' he shrugged. 'Too much competition. They're tough men and they live a tough life. And that's why' ... he looked around them ... 'we run a tough caff.' That's how he pronounced it. Deliberately, she knew. C-a-f-f.

Caff. She almost choked on it. But she was to have a little tea room. Pretty decor. Dainty dishes. Discerning ladies languidly pulling off white gloves as they decided between Indian or China blend. Certainly ... with another prick of tears ... not a leaf-thick black brew into which you stirred spoonsful of grey sugar.

A fat tear plopped.

He was rolling a cigarette in the backwoods style, first the whisper of dry tobacco betweeen large palms, then its insertion in a white wafer of paper, then the kneading to an acceptable shape, finally the tongue sealing the operation.

Through a second fat tear she watched the tongue and watched the man ... and hated him. He saw nothing amiss in this galvanized horror with its hideous E-A-T-S, he only saw something amiss in her. It was no use telling him how always between one and two she, and all the girls, had dreamed of a dainty tea-room of their own. He wouldn't follow her, or if he did he would not sympathize. There was no compassion in him, he was tough like this caff.

Now he was lighting the cigarette, sheltering it from a little wind that had idled into the room, then handing it to her. *He* handing it to *her*!

'I don't smo—' In surprise she did not finish it. For the

eyes that were looking down at her *did* have sympathy.

At once she was not sure of it, though. He shrugged and put the cigarette in his own mouth instead.

'As I was saying—' he resumed, but he only resumed that far. There was a noise outside that was quite unmistakable. Trucks.

'Damn.' He shrugged across at her and explained, 'Barney's gone back to the cut.'

'Cut?' she queried.

'He's a canecutter and only obliging me ... you ... when he's not needed on the sugar.'

'Can you get him back?'

'From the cane? Don't be silly. Haven't you any values?'

'It appears to me—'

'Better that you appear first, Miss Redland, *out there*.' Jonathan Saxby pointed somewhere beyond the door of the galley; it would be the eating part, she thought. 'Ask them what they want.'

'I ask them?'

'It's your caff, isn't it?'

'Yes, but – but—' She paused. 'What's the use of asking, anyhow, when it's steak?'

'Can't you count?'

'Of course I can count.'

'Then count the steaks.'

She went out, possibly shocked into it, and at once was horrified – that is if one can be horrified by business. It must have been a dozen trucks that had pulled up, but one of the drivers smiled and said that there were only five, the rest of the eaters were free loaders though they probably still wanted a feed.

'Steak?' she asked unnecessarily.

After a long womanless run they were eager to be friendly, and they counted up for her.

'Sixteen, miss, and ten sandwiches for the road.'

She nodded and went back to the kitchen.

'Sixteen—'

'I heard. You do the doorstops. The wherewithal is on the table. Don't stint the mustard pickle.'

Rowan got to work and had five done when he told her to carry in the first of the steaks. She looked with distaste at the bottle of tomato sauce, but decided it was not the time to be a crusader. She carried in the steaks, came back and collected more steaks. Came back and did it again. Again. She carried in the towers of bread and butter, the huge urn of tea. She distributed the sandwiches.

She received more money than she had at the office on pay Friday.

She watched the trucks go, waved back at the men.

'Come and sit down,' called Jonathan Saxby from the galley, 'and get one into you yourself.'

'No, thank you.'

'Don't eat as well?' he grinned.

'As well as what?'

'As well as don't like this place. Well, I hope you don't mind watching me.' He began on a large plate.

She did mind watching him. After he had munched happily a while that was quite apparent.

'I – I think I'll change my mind.'

'No law against that. Throw one on the grid.'

Rowan went to the refrigerator, took out a steak, then nervously approached the black beast.

The steak spluttered when she put it down and she felt that she was cooking as well as the meat, the heat was so intense, but she turned it successfully, dumped it on one of those plates you could have dropped on the bitumen, and came back and sat opposite the man.

'There,' he encouraged, 'was it that bad? And' . . . looking at the steak . . . 'is it?'

'It's good,' she proclaimed, tasting her cooking. But after all her trouble she couldn't eat. She was tired. Never had she been more tired. She pushed the plate aside and wondered could she prop up her eyes with the knife and fork.

'Bit tuckered, eh?'

'Yes.' She wondered next what lay beyond the kitchen. Surely there was somewhere she could sleep.

'Nope, there isn't.' He must have read her, though that should be easy enough by her drooping lids.

'Where did Uncle Tom—' she began.

'With me. That is, when he wasn't here. It's never closed. I told you. But when he did have to kip—'

'Kip?'

'Sleep, Miss Redland. Then he'd come across to Narganoo.'

'Your home?'

'Yes.'

'It sounds aboriginal. What does it mean?'

'Red.'

'Red sunsets, I suppose. Or sunrises.'

'No.'

He was on his smokes again, and she said irritably, 'Red cigarette tip. Rare red steaks.'

He laughed at that. 'Bit edgy, aren't you? Tuckered out, as I said. Get your things and I'll take you across.'

'But I can't stop there.'

'Why?'

'Why? Because for one thing—' She flushed vividly. She could feel her intense heat. Narganoo was red, he had said, and so, she knew, was she. She thought what a stiff fool she must sound to him. Up in this tall state such conventions would be unheard-of, they would be—

'You're wrong there,' he had anticipated her again. 'We're well to the fore when it comes to formality, it takes sophistication to be informal and we're still an unsophisticated place. To be brief, Miss Redland, I run to a housekeeper . . . or chaperone. Now will you come?'

She paused. 'Who will be here?'

'Barney will be back.'

'I see.' She thought a moment, but even the effort of thinking exhausted her, so she gave in. But she added, 'It would only be for the night.'

'I certainly intended only that.' He gave a hateful grin.

He got up, took the dishes to the huge sink, poured hot water on them, then left it at that. He did not bid her to come again, he simply nodded his head towards the door, and, after a slight hesitation, she got up and followed him.

Once free of the garish lights of the café, for each of the E-A-T-S was illuminated in a different gaudy hue, the night was very dark. For a moment she puzzled at the depth of that darkness, then saw that there was no street lighting.

She mentioned this to the man now beside her, and he answered, 'It's a motorway, not Main Street.'

'Where is Main Street?'

'None.'

'Well, where is the street, the street that goes through the town?'

'No town.'

'Then village . . . hamlet . . . whatever you like to call it.'

'There isn't any,' he said. 'Cosy Corner is just a place on the way up. Also' . . . he grinned . . . 'on the way down. Which is good for you.'

'You mean . . . what do you mean?' She was looking at him aghast. She previously had come to the conclusion that Uncle Tom's caff . . . there, she was saying it now . . .

that his café was a little far out, but never had it occurred to her that it was out of *nothing*.

'Well, it's yours now, isn't it,' he pointed out, 'so being situated on the up and down must make it good for you. But only, of course, so long as I, the trustee—'

'Oh, I know all that,' she burst in angrily. 'What I meant was are you actually telling me that this is all there is?'

'Of course. Why otherwise would the caff have opened?'

'They open in shopping centres.'

'Not places like Eats.'

'No.' Bitterly.

She was following him to a station waggon, getting in beside him. 'And what do you do in this place of nothing?' she asked, 'that is apart from helping out at the back there.'

'I only help in an emergency, and this was one.'

'And at other times?'

'I could cane-cut, timber-get, banana-farm, nut-raise, a dozen things,' he said proudly, proud of his district. 'However, I—'

'Look!' She stopped him in alarm. 'A fire!' Flames leapt up from a field in the near-distance, crimson flares that licked greedily as though to set alight to the sky.

'It's only a burning-off.'

'Burning-off?'

'They have to burn off the rubbish before the cut can begin.'

'Rubbish? Cut?' she queried.

'All sugar cane has a lot of unusable rubbish to be got rid of. Especially must it be stripped before a manual cut can begin. And C.C. is mainly manual, because we're in a pocket of wind weather here, and the breeze plays too much havoc for the mechanical cutter, it makes diabolical shapes of the yield which the machine dislikes.'

'So it's cut by hand?'

'Yes.'

'A slow process.'

'Barney,' he said deliberately, 'alone can account for eleven tons a day.'

That, and the crimson beauty of the burning-off, silenced her for a while. 'It's pretty,' she said of the fire.

'And good to be away from. The mice run out, the rats, the sugar 'roaches, a snake upon occasion, giant cane toads that sit at six inches, only' . . . a laugh . . . 'they'll be hopping from the flames, possibly on to you. No, you wouldn't like it.'

They were on the motorway now. The trucks were only intermittent, she noted. Rowan wondered if any of them would stop at Tom Thumb – at E-A-T-S. A hysterical little laugh caught at her throat.

'Did you say something?' he asked.

'Then you're not cane, timber, bananas?' she averted.

'No.'

'Then one of the other dozen things?'

'I don't call it one of, I call it *the*. Because this is the only district in Australia where it's raised, and the only district in all the world where it's done by European labour.' He left the motorway to start down a narrow winding track. The headlights lit up fields beyond the bordering trees on either side of the drive, and she noted that they were the same crop she had seen earlier, and not recognized.

'What is it?'

'Ginger.'

'Ginger?' She leaned out of the waggon and breathed in. There was not the sweetness she had expected, more a pungency. But perhaps the scent only came at a certain

23

stage of growth.

'White ginger blossom,' she said dreamily. It was the name of a pretty song, she remembered, as well as a pretty flower.

'Red,' he said.

'Red? But—'

'The white is the wild variety. Very bridal and very beautiful. Suitable for a maiden's ear. Correct side, of course.'

She knew he was baiting her, and said stiffly, 'So this is different?'

'Totally different. Chalk to cheese, and our red is the cheese.'

'*Your* opinion.'

'All the growers. All the consumers. All the economists.'

'Man doesn't live by bread alone.'

'Well, he doesn't live at all on white ginger blossom. This ginger is controlled.'

'Which would clinch it for you.'

'Certainly. Everything should be controlled.'

'Particularly women.' She did not know why she said that unless it was the bitter realization that of all the trustees she could have won herself, she had won this one. This Jonathan Saxby.

For a moment he took his eyes off the track winding endlessly, it seemed, through the ginger crop.

'Particularly women,' he agreed. 'Incidentally' . . . they were still travelling the private road which must be a long track and crossing a large estate . . . 'you asked me about Narganoo.'

'Red.'

'Yes. It's Narganoo for the ginger, actually the red shoot of the ginger, for there is really very little flower.'

'And you named the house after it?'

24

'My – grandmother did.' There was a slight pause in his reply.

'Your family has been here since?' Rowan said incredulously. Surely people couldn't live on ginger.

Again, to her annoyance, he read her mind. 'Tell me,' he demanded, 'what do you know about the uses of ginger?'

She hesitated. Ginger pudding. Ginger in fascinating stoppered bottles at Christmas.

'I thought so,' he said as she did not answer.

They must be coming to a homestead, though it was difficult to see in the dark, all that the headlights seemed to illumine was a winding track set in crops. But this last bend seemed to twist in a complete circle, and Rowan waited for the conclusion. It came all at once with one of the houses she had noted already in Queensland. Large, sprawling, set on piles for coolness, rimmed by wide verandahs. There would be frangipanni, she thought, bougainvillea and hibiscus. Terra-cotta earth.

'Narganoo,' he announced, and drew up the waggon. Then he put his finger on the horn and left it there.

The noise considerably annoyed Rowan. When he was not answered, he took the finger off, then began again.

Now the racket angered her. She said stiffly, 'If this is your method of summoning someone it appears you have a poor system of control.'

'No,' he said idly, a little amusedly, amused at her irritation, 'just a too-busy staff probably out of earshot.'

'At this time of evening? Do you work them the same hours as the Tom Thumb keeps open?'

'It is harvest,' he said laconically, 'and harvest means a lot of things to be done in a short time. None of these things evidently answering the boss's call.'

'You, of course, are the boss.'

'Of course.'

'The boss who controls?' It was a sarcasm, for there was still no response to his summons.

'Of course,' he said again. He gave Rowan a quick glance, then indicated, 'Here comes one of my controlled ones now. My housekeeper ... and your chaperone ... Nancy. Nancy, this is Rowan Redland, niece of old Tom Thumb. How's the peeling going?' He turned to Rowan and explained, 'Every individual ginger root has to be hand cut.'

'For the same reason as the district's cane?' she asked. 'The wind?'

'No, wind doesn't come into it, only excess fibre which is fatal in the final product.' He turned again to the older woman.

'The peeling,' reported Nancy, 'is going all right, though some of the new girls don't seem to be getting the feel of the grading.'

'Seasonal workers,' the man told Rowan, 'up from Melbourne and Sydney.' There was a faint scorn in his voice and Rowan wondered how much more scornful he was of someone from England.

But if he was scornful, Nancy was welcome itself. She was very brown – all her freckles had joined up, she told Rowan as she led her along to one of the many rooms; these Queensland houses, Rowan thought, were certainly capacious.

'Sun is pleasant, but it leaves its mark. When I look at a fair skin like yours ...' she sighed.

'I'll be a redskin next week,' said Rowan. 'That range in the restaurant ...'

'That reminds me,' broke in Nancy urgently, 'I must set out the late shift supper. We're working just now on an overseas consignment.'

'Is the factory in the grounds, then?'

'Right in this building you could say, though you can't

26

see it from your window, you can only see the crop. Make yourself comfortable, love, then join us in the common-room. You'll find it from the chatter.'

Rowan found a bathroom first, and washed her hands, slicked a comb through her acorn hair. Then she sought out the chatter.

She stood a little shyly at the door, but not for long. She was greeted by girls, now taking off their aprons or overalls, finishing a day's work with a cup of tea and scones spread lavishly with what looked like a golden conserve.

'Ginger marmalade,' said Nancy by her side, 'one of our best sellers. Up here at Narganoo it's all ginger. You'll understand it better tomorrow, love, and after you've been here a few days . . .' But Rowan doubted that, for she had no intention of stopping longer than the one evening. She recalled, a little vexedly, that he, too, Jonathan Saxby, had been anxious about that. However, she smiled at Nancy and said she supposed she would.

She went to sleep that night with a pungent smell in her nostrils. She dreamed that she had opened a small tea room, and ladies were coming in and choosing delicately between cakes and pastries, but when she brought the tray to the table, it held steak. It held corned beef doorstops of sandwiches. It held—

'Rise and shine!' The man, quite unabashed, put the tray on the bedside table, said, 'Half an hour, Miss Redland, Barney will want to be on the cut by eight,' and went out.

There was a pot of tea (and when she poured it was actually amber and there were no leaves). There was thin toast with the golden ginger conserve she had eaten last night.

There was also . . . and she had to smile at the thought of that man, that man who rolled backwoods cigarettes

27

and called the café caff doing it . . . a sprig of ginger blossom, more a red shoot as he had said. But of course it was for her examination, nothing else.

She took it up, felt it, sniffed it. She was still considering it when somewhere a clock chimed, and she hastily finished the tea, snatched a shower, dressed in as suitable an attire as she could find for a caff called Eats, then, as a finger touched a horn, she went down the hall and out of the house to the waiting waggon.

He was sitting behind the wheel, and he said, 'It may be a poor method of control, Miss Redland, but it certainly gets results.' He grinned.

'I was thinking of everyone's ears,' she came back coldly.

'Only think of yourself,' he advised. 'Because I won't be making allowances for you when I judge how you make out.' He had started down the drive, but he looked at her a quick hard moment.

'You understand?' he said.

'In short the ginger, not the gingerbread man,' she taunted. 'Expect no moderation. Make it hard and hot.'

'Our early crops are quite the opposite, they're soft and mild.'

'Not like the boss.'

'I'm glad you recognize my position.'

'To your *staff*,' she came back.

'In a way you are too,' he reminded her. 'Either you please me, or out you go.'

'My café pleases you, you mean.' She took care to avoid 'caff'. '*I* have nothing to do with you.'

'Only as the man who says yea or nay,' he inserted.

'You like your position, don't you?'

'I never did like it. I told Thommo so. Now I like it even less.'

'Because of me?'

'Can you roll a cigarette?'

'Because of me?' she repeated stubbornly.

'Steer while I roll one myself.' She did and he did. Then: 'Yes.'

'Thank you!'

'You're welcome. You're also an angry red. It shows like a flag in a skin like yours.'

'Is that annoying you now? My skin?'

'You've got it wrong. I'm not annoyed at your skin, nor your angry flesh. Red is my favourite colour.'

'Narganoo,' she said. They were coming out of the gate now and turning on to the motorway. The name of the house was imprinted over a large entry arch.

'Yes, Narganoo . . . red.' He was putting his foot down on the accelerator, going much faster, surely, than was necessary. 'Trucks coming,' he grinned at her. 'Could be customers.'

He got to Eats only a few minutes before the hauliers did. Rowan barely had time to button on an apron.

'Six s. and e.'s,' he called. 'Two bundles of sandwiches. Barney will be in at four. Meanwhile' . . . a slightly mocking bow . . . 'it's all yours.'

As he left she heard another truck pulling in.

CHAPTER TWO

Two hours later Rowan surfaced again, or that was what it seemed to her after she had waved the last breakfast truck away and had stood longer than she should, for there were dishes in the sink awaiting her attention, breathing in the warm silky air.

One truck had followed the other, and the steaks had been flung on the grill in quick succession, the eggs had spluttered in the pan. In between she had piled bread and butter in the Towers of Pisa she had noted yesterday, brewed tea in immense pots, or, when several trucks had arrived at the same time, in an urn. She had been grateful to find that Barney had spent the night hours when he had not been in steak attendance in cutting and parcelling the doorstop sandwiches. Taking them from the fridge as needed, she decided that this must be a house practice. She resolved to do the same herself as soon as she had dealt with her cleaning chores.

But just now she could not tear herself away from the warm silky world outside her galvanized horror. She had been too outraged to note her environs when she had arrived the previous early evening, and when she had found time, it had been to dark to see. Then this earlier a.m. Jonathan Saxby had fairly flung her into work, no opportunity for looking around. But now it was mid-morning, the rush over, a bright, clear morning, not a cloud in the wide larkspur sky, and Rowan did look around.

The countryside was very beautiful, but totally different from any beauty she had ever known. For one thing there was so much more of it, and she remembered that next to the west, this big near-tropical Queensland state contained the bulk of Australia's considerable land mass. Although this was only a corner of it ... Cosy Corner, and a rueful laugh at that ... she could sense the extent of that bulk. There seemed to be distance everywhere, and part of her own particular distance, the western part, was punctuated by the most fascinating mountains she had ever seen. They towered in odd shapes, pinnacles, domes, minarets, fingerpoints, never two alike, and they seemed to swell quite unexpectedly from a barely rising ground.

All the ground appeared cultivated except a portion fairly near her horror, since the horror occupying a slightly elevated position enabled her to see fairly fully over the near and distant environs, and the covering, she saw, was the rich lush same as she had noted yesterday ... cane, timber, fruit, nuts, and that crop she knew now, ginger.

The uncultivated portion, though still well covered in grass, was just beyond a near thicket of gum, and as it seemed left undressed deliberately she wondered what it was.

She turned her eyes next to the motorway, that road between two points where things had to get up and down ... 'and glad T.T. is about that' ... and noted that just now there was nothing to be glad about, for the bitumen was absolutely empty. It must be the in-between lull, only very late breakfasters or very early lunchers could be expected, but it didn't worry her, not with all those takings in the till, more in several hours than she previously had earned in a week. Was that the way Jonathan Saxby wanted it? The will had said 'carried on in the manner it is now being transacted' but the will had also made Jonathan the judge. It made it difficult, Rowan thought; Jonathan Saxby might want nothing changed, on the other hand he might require changes that he considered Uncle Tom would have incorporated in the course of time had he lived, those changes everyone makes with progress. It all added up finally to what *he* thought, that ginger man who was Uncle Tom's trustee, and the fact of her absolute dependence on him riled Rowan.

Particularly of her immediate dependence. For between customers she had edged in time to examine the horror, and, unless you counted a dilapidated sofa, there was nowhere to sleep. There was a corner she could clean out, but that would take time, and she must have a bed. Where, in this place of nothing, did you buy a bed? Uncle Tom had kipped, as the ginger man put it, at Narganoo, but she wouldn't again, not after that cool 'I only intended the night' of his in reply to her objection. She would sooner sleep on the motorway, and judging by the emptiness of it right now she could.

She noted for the first time a cleared section leading from the motorway to somewhere she could not see even from this elevation, but knew that she wanted to. It veered in from the bitumen almost opposite to the horror, and, unable to resist the temptation, Rowan looked up and down again, saw no customers in sight, no distant traffic, so she darted across. The clearing could be like the drive to Narganoo, go on for miles, but she still had to see. She ran down the root-rutted surface for perhaps some hundred yards ... then caught her breath at a sudden unfolding of distant flag-blue sea. It lay far below her, for they were well above sea level, and it would be the Pacific Ocean, those lilac islands she could see mistily in the horizon would belong to part of the Great Barrier Reef. She stood entranced. Several times in the rush this morning she had felt she had known a different smell than browning beef, but never had she put it down to the tang of the sea. Mountains, ocean, with a lush layer between of sugar, nuts and ginger, how quite perfect this all was, and how she wanted to stop. But how . . . resentfully . . . could she with a Jonathan Saxby? Besides, man does not live by bread alone . . . *and a woman does not live on steak*. Rowan knew if she was to stop here that as well as satisfy Jonathan she had to satisfy herself. She did not mind conceding some of the things she had planned . . . the little aprons on the fresh girls, for instance, the pretty music . . . but she had to have some self-expression. All the takings in the world would not cancel that. The takings! She had left the takings in the till! Turning away from the shouting blue, Rowan raced along the clearing.

To her dismay a car was pulled up. She would have preferred a truck. Already she believed she knew the ways of trucks. Their drivers would be sluicing themselves from the large iron dish under the tank under the big mango tree . . . that was one of the improvements she yearned to achieve, a proper amenity . . . waiting for the Eats proprietor to bring out the eternal s. and e.'s, or the mustard pickle doorstops, rather glad, in spite of the fact that time was money, for a break. These truckies, Rowan sensed already, were under deep strain.

But cars she did not know, neither what their drivers ordered, now how far they walked into a caff . . . café . . . well, her restaurant, anyway, where right now the till was left unlocked. She remembered hold-up films she had seen, and advanced nervously, rather anticipating a stockinged face pushed into hers, something cold and menacing stuck in her ribs.

The face was not stockinged and the something cold was a bottle of lemonade that the intruder . . . she knew from the coins piled on the counter that it should be cus-tomer, not intruder . . . had served himself. 'Hullo,' he said, 'you really should leave out an honesty box.' He held up the cordial and smiled.

Rowan smiled back.

'I should have been in attendance,' she apologized, 'but I simply couldn't resist that clearing across the motorway. Was there anything else you wanted?'

'Yes.' He crinkled his eyes at her and she liked the friendly boyish look. 'The reason why a native suddenly has the urge to look down on her tramping ground, however lovely. It's said that familiarity blurs appreciation.'

'It couldn't,' she denied, seeing again that sudden impact of shining blue. 'Anyway,' in explanation, 'I'm new.'

'Very new,' he agreed warmly, eyeing the fresh youth of her. He amended hastily, 'I mean . . . well . . .' He finished anxiously, 'It was intended as a compliment.'

'And accepted as one,' she reassured him. 'I'm only surprised that you could speak like that of that. It could never be familiar.' She waved her hand to where she knew now the Pacific Ocean would lie shimmering in the bright sun.

'Ah, but I'm new, too. In fact, I haven't gone down that clearing, either. Oh, I know, of course, I'm near the sea . . . the Sunshine Coast, this is called, incidentally, fellow newchum, as opposed to the Gold Coast farther down, the Capricornian farther up . . . but so far I haven't examined it. I don't suppose' . . . eagerly . . . 'you could show it to me.'

'I've already been absent without leave,' she apologized.

'You're employed here?'

'No, I'm the owner.'

'Then—?'

'But only if I satisfy,' she admitted. 'It's a long story, with, if I don't do everything I should, a sad ending.'

'It sounds interesting, and as the lady sleeps' . . . he waved towards the car where evidently there was a passenger, but Rowan could see no evidence . . . 'I'm not in a hurry. So can't I be told?'

Rowan peered speculatively at him. Although she had been in Queensland only a short time and could not really judge, to her he did not look a Queenslander. An Australian, yes, but not the rangier, more leisurely type she had noticed up in this northern state, men who moved in a different way, a looser more relaxed way, who spoke in a slower, easier tone. Sun men, she had thought. This man was more what she would imagine the crisper south would produce.

She saw he was waiting, and said, 'I can't see how the story could interest a passer-through. Unless, of course, you're a writer and collect such things.'

'I'm not a passer-through, I'm a comer-to. And I'm not a writer, I'm a vet. At least, I'm qualified, though I haven't practised yet.'

'And you're going to?'

'Not exclusively. This property that I . . . we . . . have inherited—'

'More inheritors! I hope you haven't landed a trustee as well.'

'No, it's unconditionally mine . . . at least ours.'

'Your wife's, too?'

'No wife, a sister, who has agreed to come in this thing with me. Elissa is my only worry. I only hope she'll settle down.'

'Then she isn't a vet as well? I mean if she was you wouldn't be worrying.'

'I'm not really worrying,' he admitted, 'well, not overly. All Elissa wanted was Out, out of her previous existence, and this is very out after Melbourne.'

'She was tired of it?'

'She was tired of a love affair. They both were. The inheritance occurred at almost the same time, so

35

here we are.'

'What kind of stud have you inherited? I've heard of the Brahman cattle up here, and how the breeding is flourishing.'

'Only the property came to us,' he related. 'It was from a distant relative. The stud is my idea. Not cattle, horses. I can't see why I ... we ... shouldn't succeed. It's not the accepted Irish mist climate, I'll concede, but it's still the lovely silky air that horses like. Anyway' ... a smile ... 'horses were the only thing to win Elissa over, I mean apart from that Out she so urgently wanted. She's a real pony girl.' He looked at Rowan. 'You are, too, no doubt. There's a rapport between a girl and a horse that—'

'Haven't you noticed an accent?' Rowan came in slyly.

'I thought it was the Australians who had the accent, but yes, of course I'd concluded that you were English, but all the more reason surely that you would be an animal girl, I mean if not horses, then dogs, then failing dogs—'

'Foxes,' she laughed.

'You hunted?'

'Typed. The quick brown fox jumped over the lazy dog. No, I'm afraid you're looking at a townie. A London townie.'

'Name of?' he pleaded, and again he had that winning boyish look.

'Rowan Redland.'

'I'm Nicholas Jarvis.' He put out his hand and she took it at once.

'But you like horses?' he appealed, having reluctantly taken his hand away only after Rowan had withdrawn hers.

'Oh, yes. Who doesn't? But I wouldn't be like your sister, I mean I'd be no asset in a stud.'

'Neither will Elissa be much asset. She simply likes to ride in attractive gear, emphasis on attractive. Oh, no' ... a shrug and a resigned smile ... 'help was not the purpose.'

'I remember,' Rowan nodded, 'it was Out after a tired love affair.'

'And the beginning, I hope, of a new one, with someone unsophisticated this time, not like the smart crowd she's been mixing with. Elissa grew up too quickly, she went through things too quickly. I want her to slacken off, to find new values. I want' ... he looked carefully at Rowan as though to assess her reaction to his scheme ... 'Elissa to marry up here. A cane grower, a timber fellow, a—'

'What's wrong with a gingerbread man?' At his plainly astonished look, Rowan amended, 'Ginger, I mean, without the bread. Ginger is a flourishing crop.'

He seemed relieved that she was not scandalized at his disclosure. 'I've heard of the ginger,' he said. 'Are there any ginger possibilities, or are you too new to know?'

'I'm very new, in fact only a day old, but there is an offering, and, by appearances, quite a lucrative one.'

'Lucre is an asset but not an essential. He sounds quite a boy.'

'A man.'

'Of course, you said so – the gingerbread man.'

'I leave out the bread,' she reminded him. 'With the bread he sounds kind and rather folksy, which he is not, I mean not to me, though he's probably quite reasonable to anyone else, that is' ... remembering ... 'if you obey on the double. But he's not' ... she said again ... 'to me. You see, I'm at a disadvantage. He's that trustee.'

'The possible reason for that sad ending you haven't time to tell me?'

'Yes,' she said. She added, laughing, 'You're getting a

37

lot for someone who's not to be told.'

He laughed back.

'Are you just arriving?' she inquired. 'And where is the stud?'

'I've examined it before, of course, but not "arrived" before. This is a first time for Elissa.' He frowned, and Rowan knew that he was a little worried in spite of that 'not overly' of his. 'There's no company for my sister,' he said.

'I'm here.'

'Yes, and you're a sight for sore eyes. But even though you're only through the bush' . . . he pointed and Rowan knew now what that break of the trees she had wondered over was . . . 'it's still not company in the house. Elissa is used to house company. Because I was fulfilling a scholarship abroad, and our family were all gone, Elissa lived in a hostel, a female one.'

'So did I.' But rather different, Rowan judged, glancing at the fairly expensive car and guessing that even a humble stud would need money, from Miss Grimbell's.

A sudden thought struck her, a sudden hope, and almost as though he read her mind, he asked, 'Where are you living?'

'Well . . .' she began.

She told him more of her story, of her stay last night at Narganoo, of her intention not to go back.

'But where to go?' she admitted. 'I can fix up something here, but what do I do until I've done the fixing? I mean, we're miles from town.'

'The truckies would always bring you anything in,' he said, 'but perish the thought.'

'Why? I've found them very good. Most generous and co-operative.'

'I agree, Rowan, but perish that thought when only some hundred yards through the bush the stud with a bungalow with no less than five bedrooms – yes, that's right – awaits.'

The prospect was pleasing . . . as well as being the only answer until she could fix up a corner of her own, but Rowan went carefully. 'I would want more than a room to await me,' she admitted, 'I mean . . . that is . . .'

'*I* await.' Rowan had not heard the girl approaching, had not seen her standing there listening, and now she turned to one of the prettiest faces she had seen, a little petulant perhaps, but only childishly so, as though she had not quite grown up, for all her brother's assertion that she had grown up too quickly.

'I'm an eavesdropper,' the girl said, 'so I know a lot already. You're Rowan. I'm Elissa, and you're going to live in the house. It's just perfect. I simply couldn't face it without female company, not after the gang at Eight Arundel Gardens, not straight off.' She came across holding out her hand.

'It's awfully good of you,' Rowan tried to say, but the brother and sister gave her no opportunity for thanks.

'It's all settled, then. Will you come across now?'

'I can't leave the horror. I mean Tom Thumb . . . Eats, not until Barney takes over. At any moment the lunch rush should begin.' Even as she said it, a truck pulled up, the driver and offsider calling as they made their way to the dish of water under the mango for *double* s. and e.'s. 'Driven right through the border,' they called cheerfully.

Elissa was plainly unwilling to leave, and Rowan thought that her brother would have no trouble interesting her in new faces, male style, but Nicholas was anxious to get to the homestead, and bundling his sister in, he backed out the car, calling to Rowan that they would see her later. *And not to change her mind.*

If Rowan had had any idea of doing that, a cruising car

some hours later (three trucks, rearguard of a score of others who had stopped, filled and departed, still pulled up outside Eats) would have fortified her. Jonathan Saxby, trustee, on the prowl, seeing if everything was being carried on in the manner it should be. On an impulse, Rowan picked up a pineapple that one of the previous truckies, trucking down pineapples from the north, had presented her with, sliced and grilled it with the steak. The man who received it looked surprised but still ate it.

Absurdly pleased at *some* change, anyway, Rowan worked on.

The late lunchers extended well into the afternoon, and besides pineapple, Rowan made a banana innovation in the form of a hand of bananas on every table. Why not? This was the land of such delights, of pineapples ripened in a bright sun right to their firm gold core, of big yellow bananas only cut from their palm hours before.

'Regular K.R.s, you'll be having us believe we are,' said one of the truckies, and when Rowan asked what that was, he grinned: 'Knights of the road, miss.'

He put down more money than he should have, and when Rowan objected, he pointed out that he had enjoyed extra service.

'But it wasn't done for that, I mean—' But the man was gone. Rowan stood thinking a while. She had no wish to raise her rates, Uncle Tom's rates, and she felt sure that Jonathan Saxby would have no wish, either, in fact that such a move on her part would mean a bad mark. But if a customer insisted on paying more, who was she to stop him? She separated the extra he had left, found an empty tin and placed the coins in it. Then she marked the tin 'Wash Room'. Anything over would go to improving that iron dish arrangement under the mango tree.

As the last late luncher drifted off, and she began preparing the sandwich service ahead for Barney as Barney had done ahead for her, Rowan found herself becoming quite involved in this inheritance that yesterday had so disgusted her. She mentally put up curtains, certainly not the pretty folksy ones her tea-room was to have had, but cool rattan. She played music on a record player, western style, a few manly band renditions. She supplied a desk and writing paper and pen, magazines, a fan.

There would be nothing extra charged, but if there was extra left, it would go into the tin. She felt quite excited, less unfulfilled. A car with two tourists pulling up, looking in, then going on, quickly deflated her new satisfaction bubble. She had known why they hadn't stopped. Afternoon tea drinkers would never be attracted by Eats. It wasn't s. and e. they wanted, nor corned beef doorstops, but scones and jam. Jam? What about that ginger conserve she had had last night? She stopped her doorstop filling for a while and smiled to herself. Here was a chance to flatter Jonathan Saxby and at the same time win a point for the new owner. No producer could fail to be mollified by a request to use his products.

'You look,' said a voice at the door, 'like the kitten that got the cream.'

It was her trustee, and Rowan wondered how he would have reacted had she said, 'No, but my new customers are going to get it – scones, ginger spread and cream.' But she must go slowly.

'I've been busy,' she said docilely.

'And the realization of all the money you've taken had brought that satisfied grin? Don't let it extend ear to ear, Miss Redland, it would take so much longer to wipe off. I still have the final say, remember.'

'I remember,' she nodded, still carefully docile. 'Am I to gather then that it's not just a matter of monetary success that counts?'

41

'It's not your prerogative to gather anything, except the dishes for the sink,' he said cuttingly. 'What are these bananas doing on the table?'

'I put them there.'

'I didn't think they walked.'

'No,' she agreed ... silently counting ten. 'I thought,' she proffered, 'seeing they were in the garden, that they should be used. I also' ... she might as well tell him before he discovered ... 'added grilled pineapple to Uncle Tom's menu.'

'No wonder you were purring, all that extra reward.'

'No extra reward, the prices haven't risen. Though if someone leaves more than they're obliged ...'

'You pounce on it for the kitty?'

'For the wash-room kitty. That dish under the tank is an abomination.'

To her surprise, he agreed, 'You're quite right there.' Rowan felt she had gained a few marks.

Emboldened, she said that a shower would be a good idea, after dusty miles men needed to freshen up as well as stoke. Besides, it should help in the same category as coffee and hot mustard pickle sandwiches helped.

'To keep alert? Yes, I agree.'

She was about to take advantage of his amicable mood and mention the proposed afternoon teas, adding extra softening in the proposed use of his own products, when, presumably already softened, he said rather tentatively: 'I spoke out of turn last night, about where you're to sleep, Miss Redland. Of course it must be Narganoo. Nancy is quite excited about it, and wouldn't dream of you sleeping anywhere else, even if you could ... which you can't.'

'I can.' Because of the new amiability between them she made it as casual as she could.

'Oh yes' ... a trifle impatiently ... 'I know you can rig

42

up a cot here, but I couldn't allow that, of course.'

'Of course?'

'Up till now we've had a remarkably safe record on this motorway, no violence, not even theft. But the world goes on.' He shrugged.

She said nothing, so he continued.

'Things could happen, the usual things that do happen, stick-ups, assaults, the rest. Finally it would have to end up with either Barney or me kipping here for your protection.'

'Which would never do,' she reminded him with maddening primness, all sweet friendship discarded.

'For the reason,' he said coldly, 'of plain man comfort. You might get the trucks to fetch you in a cot, but I don't intend to put myself out and buy one when I have a houseful already, and I won't sleep on a floor. So' . . . a gesture . . . 'the lady returns each night to Narganoo.'

'Sorry,' she intoned smoothly.

'So am I,' he said briskly, 'but it has to be.'

'It hasn't.'

'You are not to sleep here. I've just explained.'

'I heard you, and I accept your reason. But would there be any objection from the trustee at my sleeping elsewhere?'

'There is no elsewhere.'

'There's a new stud opened only a few hundred yards through the thicket.'

'Emery's old place? Yes, I did hear— But where do you come in?'

'I go there. Every night. I sleep there. Every night.'

'You damn well don't!'

'Who stops me? I mean' . . . at a look on his face . . . 'what reason stops me? This place has five bedrooms—'

'And a stud-owner.'

'Back to propriety again!' He looked thunderous, so

43

before he could explode she added to his stud-owner: 'There's a sister.'

That deflated him. He stood a moment, then wheeled around. 'I'll see for myself,' he said.

Rowan called sweetly, 'Do.'

The early tea trucks ... it should really be dinner trucks, but everyone here seemed to call lunch dinner and dinner tea ... were beginning to pull in, and Rowan knew that Barney would be along to help her. She wondered what the arrangement was with Barney, how much she paid him, when he had time off. She knew nothing at all of this business as yet, not even from where that big freezing unit received its gargantuan steaks.

Certainly another aspect of this place that she did not know were the two quite remarkable trucks pulling up now. Unlike the other working fellows that panted in regularly they were not ducoed in the usual subdued greens and greys, but in a bright red in one instance, in the other an eye-catching orange. On one was printed: 'The Boys', on the other: 'Hang on or Bust'. Beneath both the signs, in smaller letters, was R.R.

'It means Rough Riders, miss, the name of our association. We're here for the rodeo.' The speaker was a lean young man in tight jeans and tall wide straw Bailey hat. Rowan learned later that that was what it was called. 'S. and e. for three from The Boys, for four from Hang on or Bust,' he ordered. He went to the back of The Boys and opened it up, and Rowan saw there were two horses within, and a considerable amount of saddles, bridles, ropes, blankets and feed.

'Is there a rodeo?' she asked. She added in explanation, 'I'm new here.'

'There's always a rodeo in Queensland, especially around these parts.'

'You follow them up?'

'We're professionals.' He seemed to think it explained everything, and perhaps it did if you knew what to make of it. Rowan didn't, but she determined to find out over the s. and e.'s, for they seemed clean, attractive young men.

The haulage trucks had slackened off, so she was able to spend a little time on their plates. It was not wasted; they beamed their appreciation and assured her that if they could have they would have come back every day for grub like this. There wasn't much at Round Corner.

'Where is that from here?'

'Some miles up. Yes' ... as Rowan's brows raised ... 'there's lots of "corners" in these parts, and all good rodeo country.'

'Good horse country, too?' She was thinking of Nicholas.

'Fine. It's a wonder there's not more studs.'

'There is. Well, one, anyway.' She pointed out the clearing through the trees. 'A vet has taken it over for stud purposes.'

'A vet?' They all looked at each other.

'It's what we're after,' explained the leader of The Boys. 'We have this grey and he's not the best. Larry would want him attended to. It looks like you may be having us more often after all.'

'I'm sure he's very good,' said Rowan eagerly, eager for trade as well as keen for Nicholas. 'Why don't you go and see him?'

'We'll do just that.' They marched off in a group.

After they had gone, Rowan cleared up, smiled at the more than necessary amount left by their plates, a common occurrence now, and put the extra in the tin. Then she went out and looked in the trucks.

The ponies in Hang on or Bust looked fighting fit, but one of the greys in The Boys seemed listless. But she was pleased to see that they all appeared clean, comfortable, well groomed and loved. She wondered who Larry was.

'Not considering adding horses to the menu?' Jonathan Saxby's dry voice brought her out of her contemplation.

She started, then said irritably, 'I was admiring them.'

'That fellow, too? He looks in need of hospitalization.'

'Probably he'll be getting it. I sent the boys to the stud.'

'*You* did!'

'Why not? With a resting pony they would have to return here at times, and they've already sampled my wares.'

'Oh, just business, eh? I thought you were doing Jarvis a good turn.'

'And why not that as well?'

'Why not?' he agreed, and stood looking at her so long that she began to feel uncomfortable.

'So you saw Nic – Mr. Jarvis?' she asked.

'I saw Nicholas Jarvis. I also saw his sister.'

'Was he up to your requirements?'

'He was. So' . . . a pause . . . 'was his sister.'

'Then you approve of me stopping there until I fix up something here.' Rowan wondered why she felt so cool towards him; she did not like him, but not liking people usually only afforded an indifference to them, not a coolness like this.

'Perhaps I don't exactly approve, but I promise you I won't penalize you.'

'No doubt because of Miss Jarvis.' She could not have said why she flashed that.

It seemed to amuse him, and that made her angrier than ever.

46

'Mr. Jarvis is keen for his sister to settle here,' she said.

'That should be no trouble, she's a very beautiful girl.'

'I assured him that there was a lot of scope. I'm right, aren't I? Queensland has a lot more males ... isn't it a surplus of some two hundred thousand?'

'You've been doing your homework,' he said hatefully.

'I've been doing nothing of the sort, I simply happened to read that. I mean when you're coming to a place the least you can do is read it up.'

'The least,' he agreed maddeningly.

With an effort, for she felt like pursuing the subject, putting him in his place, but how could one put one's boss in his place, she said, 'The cane farmers were mentioned, the timber growers, the—'

'Ginger men?'

'Are there? I mean are there more than you?' Somehow she had seen him as the only ginger figure. It had been his cool self-satisfaction, she thought.

'Several.' He must have read her thoughts, and he said it thinly. 'So you didn't mention us g's?'

'I did, except in the singular, and—'

'Yes?'

'I said gingerbread. Correcting it at once, of course. Ginger you are, but gingerbread never.'

'You mean no gilt?'

'Guilt with a U?'

'How smart we are today! Money in the personal kitty as well as the till' ... he had taken up and was rattling the tin ... 'and a sharp tongue.'

'I told you the money was for—'

'Yes,' he interrupted, 'and I told you I agreed to that. I also agree to you bedding at the Jarvises'

47

for the time being.'

'In fact no points lost?'

'Not so far.'

'Even when I serve a few extras?'

'No, I can see your point there. I think old Tom would have seen it. Times change, and with competition—'

'Am I to have competition?'

'I believe it's likely.'

It seemed a likely time to mention the music, the fan, the desk, the other side of the café that would deal with teas, all the things she had been thinking about. But he gave her no opportunity.

'I've a lot to go through with you, Miss Redland ... Barney's wages, supplies ... steaks just don't appear in that freezer, you know ... but Barney will tell you as you go along, and when I have an opportunity I'll go over it again. Just now, as you must have seen last night, the business is flat out, I haven't a moment to myself.'

'I,' she said apologetically, for the rush today had given her an appreciation of how being busily occupied every moment was a robber of time, 'arrived at a wrong moment.'

She had made the statement, so why was she so angry when he agreed blandly and turned on his heel to go across to his car?

'Sleep well tonight, Miss Redland. You can see with a place like this you need to.' He got into the car.

'You, too,' she called impertinently, 'in your ginger caper.'

'Capers are hot, my ginger is not. I select only the immature plants, which gives a product with only mild, palatable heat.' He was smiling blandly, undoubtedly, she thought unfairly, emulating his wretched mild ginger. 'Of course,' he went on, 'we harvest the matured plants for extractions, flavours, essences and medicines later on.

You must come and see, Miss Redland.'

'Must?' It was out before she realized, and she bit her lip. Must to a trustee who was watching her every move.

'You almost got yourself a bad mark there,' he said quite amiably, 'but I'll waive it this time. After all, you haven't actually refused.'

'Not actually,' she agreed chokily, for she felt very close to tallying up a whole heap of adverse marks and it was hard holding back.

His revving of the car saved her . . . that, and the return through the thicket of The Boys and Hang on or Bust. Rowan saw his waggon burning up the motorway as he hurried back to his ginger factory, and knew that just at present when it came to moods she was in the extraction class that was garnered hot and matured, not mild and green. But the rodeo boys' smiles soothed her, and she listened to their plans to leave Grey here and come down frequently to check him. 'And eat with you,' they promised.

They added, 'Larry willing, of course.'

She watched as they removed the sick pony and led him along the track. She waved them away after they had returned again, put rodeo tickets in her hand, then set off.

One thing, she thought, there wasn't much time for introspection here, for wondering what it was all about. A car was pulling up now. Would the driver want tea, would he just look around, then go on?

He didn't, because he was Barney, Barney in a battered old model. Rowan followed him inside the horror, showed him her sandwich preparation for the night, other preparations, then sat him down.

'Mr. Saxby has no time, Barney, so you'll have to tell me. I want to know all about Eats.'

CHAPTER THREE

BARNEY had a leather-dark face and his eyes were deep in the creases formed from years in the glittering Queensland sun. The little eye slits you did manage to glimpse were as larkspur blue as these Queensland skies, and they were bright and friendly.

Automatically Rowan threw a steak on to the grid, sealed the juices, turned it, turned it again. At the last turn she broke in the eggs, put on the thick slice of pineapple to golden-brown it each side, then dished the whole on one of the plates you couldn't have broken with an axe.

Barney was as unsurprised at being served a meal as most people would be being served a cup of tea, but he was surprised at the pineapple. He said he thought it was a fine idea, though, and from someone like Barney who spent more hours at Eats than anyone else, it was good praise.

Rowan fired at once: 'How much do I pay you? When do I pay you? If you work all day on the cane and all night at Eats, when do you sleep? Why are you so good?'

Barney answered in rotation: 'The awkward wage. Every Friday. I don't work all day and by the same token I don't work hard like I used to, also I kip between night customers on the sofa, for sometimes it can go two or three hours between trucks.'

'You never answered,' smiled Rowan, 'why you were so good. But tell me your own way.'

Barney finished his plate, accepted black tea and coarse sugar, and lit a pipe.

'I've been cutting all my life, Miss Redland.'

'Rowan, please, Barney.'

'Rowan,' he agreed, narrowing the narrowed blue slits, if such was possible, to mere chinks, yet friendly chinks.

'You're a good cutter,' reported Rowan from Jonathan, 'eleven tons a day.'

'In my heyday,' sighed Barney, 'but now I'm getting on. So I cut much less, sometimes none at all, and do other cane jobs. There's always lots of jobs with cane. Clearing up, burning off, driving the tram . . . that tram's actually a miniature rail truck . . . to the crush. So that's why I can do with less sleep, miss, I mean Rowan. In the old eleven-ton days I used to bed down by seven.'

'I see,' nodded Rowan. She asked politely if it was because he wanted to make more money that he had taken on this extra job.

Barney did not answer that for quite a while, then he said a little uncomfortably: 'No, not exactly. You see, I had reckoned I'd like it for myself later on. I had that in mind. I thought I could have done this when I got too old even for the side jobs of the cane.'

'Oh,' said Rowan, sensing the immense disappointment he must have experienced when Uncle Thomas had died leaving a last will and testament that said '. . . to my niece.' Impulsively she leaned over and patted the leather-brown hand.

The blue slits twinkled at her. 'Don't be sorry,' said Barney. 'I'm not. Not now.'

'Now?' she queried.

'I reckon now that a man should do a thing like this for his own, that he should pass it on, as Thommo has. I didn't think so before, not with those other nephews and nieces of his, but you . . . well, you're different. You know what?' . . . another narrowing and twinkling . . . 'I'd do it, too. With you.'

'But that's wonderful,' appreciated Rowan, quite touched. 'What's made you feel like that about me?'

'I guess it was the sandwiches,' mumbled Barney, 'all bundled up nice and ready like I do myself.' He looked embarrassed, but he still smiled warmly, and Rowan smiled back. They were friends.

'You said the "other nephews and nieces". Have you met them?'

'No, I've not met them,' Barney answered, 'but they've all been here at one time or other, sucking up to old Thommo, spending his money before they got it. He woke up in the end, and I think if he hadn't died when he had, he would have altered that will.'

'Cut me out?'

'I don't know about that, but I do know he wouldn't have left it to them had you failed with it. But he went before he could alter it, and wills are wills.'

... And Jonathan Saxby, thought Rowan, is Jonathan Saxby.

'Do my cousins live near?' she asked.

'Too near,' Barney grunted.

'You mean they actually *do*.' Rowan tried out this new feeling of relationship, a relationship that she never had known before. Her father, an only child, had died in her infancy, and her mother had told her extremely little about her Australian connections. Rowan had rather gathered that when she had married and gone to England, she had been dropped by them. She smiled slightly. It was reversing the usual order, she thought.

'Where?' she insisted from Barney.

'I didn't say where, I said too near, and I mean too near, wherever it is. It's always too near when you're pestered like they pestered your Uncle Tom.'

'But *why*?' Rowan was looking around the galvanized horror, and wondering how anyone could covet it. But then something often happened to people when they thought they might benefit through a will, though she still could not understand it . . .

'It has future,' said Barney definitely. 'Queensland is the tomorrow state.'

The tomorrow state . . . Rowan liked that. I'm part of tomorrow, she thought, and found the horror a trifle less horrible.

'They all came at him,' went on Barney.

'My cousins?'

'Yes.'

'At Uncle Tom?'

'Yes.'

'All together?'

'No, in singles. But I wouldn't put it past them to unite now. In fact, I think they have.'

'How do you mean, Barney?'

Barney nodded his head cryptically towards Eats' door, towards what lay beyond the door. To the clearing. 'Opposition,' he said.

'The bus driver mentioned that. Mr. Saxby did. But do you think it would be *them*?' Rowan spoke conspiratorially as befitted Barney's conspiratorial mood.

He nodded back.

'But where would that get them?'

'They'd know the terms of the will as well as we know them. They'd know you'd have to succeed or get out.'

'But if I made a success, and I do intend to make a success—'

'Look, Rowan,' Barney explained, 'this place has a tomorrow, but you can't foist tomorrow on today. What I mean is, it will come, but not yet. What I really mean is, there's enough for one but still not enough for two.'

'Then why would my cousins do such a silly thing . . . that is if they are doing it?'

'Is one of your cousins called Pearce Grant?'

'Let me see.' Rowan went quickly in her mind down the page of her mother's Bible. 'Yes,' she said. 'There is a Pearce.'

'That's the name. Pearce Grant. Well, he's opening up on that cleared block across the road.'

'But *why*?' Rowan asked again. 'It's this place you tell me that he . . . that they want, not a new venture.'

'By opening the new venture they'll get the old one, because, as I said, though there's plenty for one, there's not enough for two. When Jonathan comes to sum it all up on profit and loss, which, being Jonathan, he'll do, because he always does things the right way, and because that was what the will said, it said profitably—'

'And beneficially,' Rowan inserted, but Barney went on.

'Then,' he finished, 'he'll have to rule against you, improvements or not, if the income has gone down. Which it would. Now do you see?'

'Yes,' said Rowan sadly, 'I see. But' . . . hopefully . . . 'miracles can happen, and if I run this place so perfectly that no one will want to try the place over the road—'

'They always do,' said Barney, 'it's human nature.'

'I can still try.' Rowan's lip was trembling a little. For someone who only as short a while ago as yesterday had looked around her and felt sunken, she had come to want this horror.

'You do that, girl,' advised Barney. 'I tell you what else you can do, you can take off and leave it now to me. You look all in.'

'It has been a long day,' Rowan admitted, 'but a remarkable day, too.' She gathered up a few things. 'If you get busy, I mean very busy, Barney, you can always call me.'

'Right out to Narganoo?'

'At the stud along the track. I'm kipping ... I'm sleeping there.' Rowan added formally, remembering Jonathan's statement of lack of convention being only for big cities, 'The new man ... *and his sister* ... have invited me.'

Barney did not comment on that. All he asked was, 'Did you remember mustard pickle on the sandwiches?'

'Yes.'

'All right then, hop off. Keep your eyes peeled on the track. Joe Blakes sometimes come out in the evening to feel the warm dust under their bellies.'

'Joe Blakes?'

'Snakes.' At her look of alarm, he assured her, 'They don't want to be stepped on by you any more than you want to be bitten by them. You'll be jake.'

'I'll be jake,' hoped Rowan, making a lot of noise as she walked along the short bush track so that any belly-warming visitors would be alerted and have time to slide away before she came on the scene.

A turn in the track brought the homestead in view. It wasn't as large as Narganoo, but of the same Queensland type. All the lights were on, although it was barely dark, and Nicholas must have been watching for her, for he came down the steps at once.

'This is jolly good of you, Rowan.'

'I was about to say the same myself about you. But for you offering this I'd be out at the gingerbread house again.'

'A gingerbread house sounds fascinating.' Elissa had come out on to the verandah. 'Is his name Hansel? Is he after a Gretel?'

'No. He's Jonathan, Jonathan Saxby. He's my late uncle's trustee.'

'How interesting for you,' Elissa said.

'I find it anything but that at present. My fate depends

55

on him.'

'Mostly women's fates do depend on men,' said Elissa a little abruptly, and Rowan thought: A story here.

'Come in,' Elissa invited. 'It's all still a mess, but what can you expect?'

The place was spacious, large rooms, many of them. The early Queenslanders might not have bothered with design, but they had bothered with fellow comfort. There was room to move, to breathe, to relax. Rowan said so.

'I find it all a little primitive,' shrugged Elissa, 'but it has its points.'

Nicholas began thanking Rowan for sending along the rodeo boys. Elissa sparkled, too, at that.

'Can you do anything for the sick grey?' Rowan asked.

'I'm sure I can.'

'In a way,' Rowan confessed, 'it was an advantage for me, too. They've promised to eat at Tom Thumb's every time they come to check the pony. That is,' she recalled, 'if Larry O.K.s all this.'

'Larry?' It was Elissa, and sharply.

'That's what was said.'

'Larry,' Elissa repeated thoughtfully. 'Not a usual name.'

'Yet not unusual,' pointed out Rowan. 'I rather gathered he was the big boss of the outfit.'

'Rodeos are part of the Queensland scene,' came in Nicholas, 'so a big boss would be needed.'

'But why would horses?' Rowan asked. 'I mean I thought these daredevil riders just climbed on a pony's back, then that was that.'

'There are are other events at a rodeo, events that require your own mount. Camp drafts . . . that sort of thing. Elissa can tell you, she's the equestrienne.'

'It's all quite silly,' Elissa said shortly. 'I'm afraid,

Rowan, you're going to get a very poor tea.'

'After s. and e.,' began Rowan.

'S. and e.?'

'Steak and eggs, which I seem to have been doling out all day, all I would like is a cup of—' She had started to say tea, then remembered the caff tea, leaf-thick, strong, black. 'Coffee,' she said instead.

'But a drink first,' insisted Nicholas; he was really very nice. He got out glasses.

They lingered over the drinks. Rowan had the feeling that Nicholas wanted this, wanted to entertain Elissa. He was perfectly happy already, Rowan could see that, but Elissa was restless. Several times she got up and went to the door.

'It's so big,' she sighed.

'Quite right, sister, in it you could fit three ... more? ... states of Victoria.'

'It's so ... so ...' But Elissa left it at that.

They played records, talked idly, drank coffee and nibbled sandwiches ... not doorstops of beef. Then Elissa got up abruptly and said, 'I'm going to bed. Your room is at the end of the passage, Rowan. I'm afraid I haven't made up your cot.'

'Look, you've done enough already,' protested Rowan, but by now Elissa had left the room.

'No, Rowan,' emphasized Nicholas, 'you have.' He went and poured more coffee. 'You must have gathered that my sister is on the run,' he said drily. 'Otherwise she would never have come with me.'

'That tired love affair?'

He nodded. 'That didn't come off. She's not a bad kid for all that brittle exterior. That's why I'm hoping—'

'For a cane farmer. A nut grower. A—'

'Gingerbread man,' Nicholas finished. 'We met him today. Yes, Rowan, I am.'

57

'Can you tell me? I mean' . . . hurriedly . . . 'if you want to.'

'I want to a whole lot, it would help, but I don't know myself. I only know this Lawrence affair went deep, or at least so I gathered.'

'Lawrence was the man?'

'Yes. I hadn't met him, but having lived a life of Elissa I sensed that she was a deal more thrown about after it finished than following her usual affairs.'

'Had she many?'

'She had her share.' He shrugged. 'But this particular one . . .' He sighed.

'It is a pity, then,' nodded Rowan. 'So she packed up and came with you.'

'Yes. But for how long? You can't exactly call this the bright lights, and Elissa likes her lights bright.'

'She can come down to Eats. We've different colours for each letter.'

'To where?'

'To Tom Thumb. There's drivers there day and evening, though you probably weren't thinking of a K.R. future for your sister.'

He started to laugh. 'What on earth are you talking about?'

'Knights of the Road,' laughed back Rowan. 'The truckies, the hauliers. The consumers . . . and may they continue to consume . . . of my s. and e.'

'Oh, yes,' said Nicholas knowledgeably now of that, 'steak and eggs.'

'Steak and eggs,' echoed Rowan. 'For that's all they want, didn't you know?' A slight note of hysteria must have tinged her voice, for Nicholas stood up and said decisively, 'Bed for you, too, young woman. I may only be a horse doctor, but I can tell when rest is needed. The last room, I think Elissa said.'

'Thank you, doctor,' Rowan smiled.

She went down the passage, finding she was very tired, as he had said. She had a feeling that she always would be tired like this up here, it was a completely active life.

She made up the bed sketchily, comparing it ruefully to the perfect bed and the perfect room of last night. There was no doubt that that gingerbread man did himself well. She lay down, not caring that the sheets were barely tucked in, nor the blanket ... that in a temperature like this would soon be discarded, anyway ... only thrown over.

She thought of Miss Grimbell's Establishment. Of the Young Ladies. The young ladies thinking in terms of china tea and cinnamon toast, of men, if men did intrude in the scene, as polished and urbane and shaking polite heads at proffered sugar cubes, preferring to drink their amber brew as it came from the silver pot, certainly not heavily syruped with crude sugar. Business men. Town men. Not knights of the road. Not rodeo fellows. Not ... growing progressively drowsy ... ginger men.

She awoke to sunshine streaming through the window. Just as nights were instant up here, so, she expected, would mornings come with a burst. It was quite early, but the day already seemed well into its stride. She got up, regretting (but dismissing the regret immediately) the absence of a tray with toast and ginger marmalade awaiting her. And a sprig of red ginger blossom.

She found a large bathroom that had already had use. Nicholas, of course. She showered, dressed, made up sparsely as suited these latitudes, then went down the passage.

Nicholas was gone, but he had left coffee heating. She smiled appreciatively at the thought, found a jug and carried it along to Elissa's room, was told sleepily to put it down, please, then she went back, took up her things and

59

started down the track to Eats. All she needed for her inner man would be there, at Tom Thumb.

Barney was ready to go. He said it had been a quiet night and he had managed a kip. He turned off the Eats lights, built up the fire, instructed her to throw on a steak for herself because from now till ten there was always a rush and it was better to be stocked, then departed for the cut.

He was right. Four hauliers pulled in almost at once. A tabletop followed. A car pulled up and a man and a woman argued for a few minutes, the man saying that truckies knew where to eat and the woman asking eat what, then, the woman winning, going off again. Rowan was surprised at her indignation – she, who only the day before yesterday would have done the same.

Business went on briskly right into the dinner rush, it was only after the midday meal that Rowan stopped for a breather. She was glad she had taken Barney's advice to stoke up.

She came to the door with a cup of tea, pleased, though it wasn't good business, that the motorway was temporarily empty.

Yet not quite empty. A car was pulling up on the other side of the bitumen. She watched a man get out. He glanced up, saw her, then came over, medium height, medium-eyed. She responded politely to his greeting.

'Not exactly run off your feet, are you?' he smiled at her, and nodded to the empty road.

Rowan didn't like the smile very much, nor what he said, but she answered politely again, 'I've been busy. Would you like anything?'

'Yes . . . as a matter of fact.'

'Tea? Steak? Sandwiches?'

'No. What I would like is a talk with you.'

That rather surprised her. Although here only a few

60

days she had come to sum up her customers, they always said what they wanted in a direct manner, they didn't edge shyly, or slyly, it seemed to Rowan, like this man was doing.

'Please go ahead.'

'You won't like it.'

'Won't . . .' She saw light. This man must be the opposition. 'Are you—' She glanced towards where Barney had indicated the new café was to go.

'Yes.'

'Then it can't be helped, can it? I mean I can't stop you.'

'But it can be helped. And it would save a lot of trouble if we came to terms now.'

'Came to terms?'

'Two eating houses are ridiculous.'

'I agree there, but—'

'I've come to make a proposition. Strictly I have no need to, I can go straight ahead, but so much more pleasant if we do it my way, don't you think?'

'What way?'

'I'm offering you a – consideration, will we call it?'

'Call it something more honest, please.'

'Then a sum for you to – well, forget all this.'

'Forget what?'

'This business.' He nodded to Eats.

'It's a good business.'

'*Now* it is, but when you have opposition?'

'It could be good then, too.'

'But good enough?'

'How – how do you mean?'

'I mean good enough in black and white . . . or red? Red in a ledger? You see' . . . a little smile . . . 'I know the terms of Uncle Thomas's will.'

'*Uncle* Thomas! Then you must be—'

'Yes, Rowan, I'm your cousin. Not a kissing cousin, unhappily, and that realization has really saddened me, I never expected such a pretty relation as this.'

'Kissing cousin?' She stared at him stupidly, not following him.

He said, 'Your mother, my step-aunt Selina, only came with my grandfather's late second marriage, she was not a Thumb.'

'But she was, she always said so.' Selina Thumb, Mother had said. She had told Rowan how she had disliked it.

'Probably called so out of convenience, I mean in a family of Thumbs one non-Thumb could be a nuisance, but your mother, my *step*-aunt Selina, was not.'

As Rowan stood silent, he went on . . . playfully on. 'Come to think of it, not being a kissing cousin isn't so bad after all.' A significant pause. 'We're no blood relation.'

She stared at him blankly. This was something she had not known, that her mother had evidently never bothered to tell her. No wonder, she thought fairly, the cousins resented a stepsister's child inheriting before they did themselves. She would have, too.

'I – I see,' she murmured inadequately.

'I thought I did, too.' Now he was being heavily gallant. 'I thought I had no two minds about it all. By the way, Rowan, I'm Pearce Grant, son of Frances Thumb, next in the family to your own mother.' A pause. 'But now, when I meet up with you . . .' He made a step forward. He was looking at her as he had looked before.

Rowan promptly retreated a step. She didn't like him. 'You'd better confer with the rest of my step-cousins before you make any change of strategy,' she advised briefly but definitely.

Pearce Grant closed tighter an already rather tight mouth, all his good will gone. 'Very well, then, I'll put my cards on the table. I've been commissioned by the rest of the family to suggest to you to get out of this business of yours before you're obliged to get out. It could be to your advantage.'

'You mean – that sum of money?'

'Yes.'

'It would be preferable, anyway, to the – other.' There were two spots of colour on Rowan's cheeks, already hot from the big stove. She said it in a manner he could not possibly mistake.

Her step-cousin was furious, but he kept himself in control.

'We all know the unfair terms of Uncle Thomas's will,' he stated formally.

'Then knowing and feeling like you did, why didn't you oppose it legally?'

'The law can be a devious thing. Better, we all agreed, to give you a chance to retire gracefully, and by gracefully we mean—'

'With a sum of money,' Rowan nodded. She waited. 'No.'

'No?'

'That's what I said.'

'You understand what you're doing?'

'Yes.'

'You understand that though you are satisfactorily busy now, in another month—'

'Another month?' she queried.

'Less. Our plans have been drawn up, our permit passed. Perhaps you would like to see the Outlook floor scheme.' He began to unroll a sheath of papers.

'The Outlook?'

'Which I . . . we . . . have, fortunately. There's quite a remarkable view from the coast side of this motorway, which unhappily you don't get.'

He had unrolled the plan and spread it out, but Rowan did not look at it.

After a few minutes he rolled it up again. 'A pity,' he said, 'it's quite nice. Modest ... we agreed on that, seeing it will only be necessary for a short time ... *but definitely not galvanized iron with a lack of conveniences to match.*'

He waited, but Rowan still did not speak.

'Think about it, anyway,' he invited, 'think about a suitable consolation, for we can afford that if we don't have the expense of putting up this place.'

'I've thought about it already, Mr. Grant.'

'Pearce, surely.' He was looking at her in that way again.

'I've thought about it, Mr. Grant, and the answer is no. Oh, I'm aware about room for one but no room for two and how judgment must finally be made on the returns of the account book, but I think Mr. Saxby—'

'Ah, yes, Jonathan Saxby.'

Something in her step-cousin's voice brought Rowan's eyes searching his. She looked at him curiously.

'Ah, yes, Mr. Saxby,' he said again. A pause. 'I may be wrong, but I don't believe you know very much about the real state of this relationship, do you?'

'No,' Rowan admitted unwillingly.

'Then you wouldn't know that ... No, you wouldn't know, of course.'

'Know what?'

Mr. Pearce Grant was lighting a tailormade cigarette, no backwoods rolling for him. 'Did you never have any family records, my dear?'

'In a Bible,' Rowan answered, loathing his 'dear'.

'Then refer to it.'

'It's in England.'

'Then send for it. Decidedly send for it. If you are anticipating a possibly advantageous attitude from Mr. Jonathan Saxby, get it out.'

'What do you mean?' she demanded.

'Send for that record. It will intrigue you. It will also put a few things straight. And now, dear cousin, I'll leave you on that note. I see some trucks in the distance. They must stop here, for the next break is two hundred miles north. A disgusting country, really, it never knew where to stop. Now, in your England . . .' He gave a little laugh that was drowned in the sound of the revving of his car.

From then on, it was action again. During the action, Jonathan Saxby called in. Rowan watched him as she . . . expertly now . . . turned over a steak, broke in eggs at the right moment. What was there about Mr. Jonathan Saxby that caused a man like her step-cousin to say, 'Ah, yes, Jonathan Saxby?' Why had her step-cousin advised her to bring out the family Bible?

She would, of course, if only to learn about her cousins who were not that but step-cousins after all. She thought (as she piled up Towers of Pisa of bread and butter) that she could have felt deprived about those cousins had she not met, and disliked at once, Pearce Grant.

'Getting quite an expert.' Jonathan came and stood beside her.

'Is that a good point?' she asked tartly.

He hunched his big shoulders. 'I've been on the ginger all day, don't give me more now.'

She carried in a tray, came out to pile up another.

'It really doesn't matter, does it?' she said bitterly.

'What doesn't matter?'

'The good points. In the end you really have to go on results, don't you, and what chance have I when—'

'What? Discouraged this early?'

'I'm not, only it's true, isn't it, and now that that place

is opening—'

'So you know about that?'

'You hinted it to me,' she reminded him.

'Oh, yes, I knew.'

'Then why didn't you tell me definitely?'

'Perhaps I thought you'd learn soon enough.'

'You knew my – relations were doing it?'

'Yes.'

'I suppose you knew, too, that they're really not.'

He looked at her in surprise. 'Didn't you?'

'I only knew my mother was the youngest, just a little afterthought, I believed.'

'And perhaps she was.'

'Maybe, but not my *step*-grandfather's afterthought, as my *step*-cousin Pearce Grant has recently told me.'

'Oh, so he's been here.' Jonathan's eyes were narrowed.

'Not their own grandfather's afterthought and no relation really of Uncle Tom's,' repeated Rowan. 'No wonder they—'

'Rot,' came in Jonathan Saxby. 'Relationship *is* nothing, love is.'

'Love?'

'I mean ... well, I mean you can't build up something simply because you're connected.'

'He ... Pearce ... was pleased we were not connected,' said Rowan distastefully.

'Was he?' Jonathan looked sourly at her. 'And you?'

'It was a shock. I mean I didn't know. He told me to send to England for records, which I will do, of course.'

'I wouldn't,' Jonathan said.

'Why?'

'It's quite unnecessary. You've learned the true relationship, leave it at that.'

About to argue, Rowan changed her mind. She was

now determined to send over to London at the earliest possible moment, which would be as soon as Mr. Saxby finished his inspection and went out. There was something odd here, something she had to know.

The time did not come for several hours, indeed it was just before Barney took over. The motorway empty, Rowan took up the big black phone. After some vigorous ringing, there was an answer. The exchange was yet another Corner — no wonder the rodeo boys had said there were lots of corners. The telephonist listened to Rowan's cable, then said, 'But, darling, you needn't send to London for a Bible, I'll loan you one.'

It seemed to Rowan it was the first friendly human thing she had heard all day, not counting the hauliers who were always friendly, but from non-customers. She explained that it was a family Bible that she had to have, it had a page of relations.

'Yes, they can be the devil,' sympathized the telephonist, who said she was Shirley and to call on her when she came in. Came in where? Then Shirley said she would book the cable and how did she like it up here, it was all right if you had nowhere else. But it was said in the same proud tone as Jonathan had used.

Rowan put the phone down as Barney came in. He told her the next week's steaks would arrive tonight and he would stack them. They had a cup of tea together and some of the sandwiches that Rowan had found time to cut and wrap. Barney said judiciously they could have been thicker and hotter, but they weren't bad, not for a newchum.

Nodding wearily, the newchum made her way along the track, not bothering about snakes now, so she must be getting acclimatized, to the stud.

CHAPTER FOUR

S<small>HE</small> must have been earlier than yesterday evening, for it was lighter; instant night had not yet gathered together its black backdrop. On the other hand summer could be on the way, Rowan mused. Up here you'd never really know unless you consulted the calendar. She was not used to seasons that held hands with each other, but she found it very pleasant . . . apart from the snakes that Barney had warned her of . . . to feel soft warm earth beneath her.

She turned the bend of the track to see that Elissa was out on the sick grey, who now appeared vastly improved, which was something, Rowan smiled, for Nicholas's skill. Both horse and girl obviously were enjoying themselves, and Elissa looked radiant. She was the perfect equestrienne, and undoubtedly aware of it. No hurried jeans and jumper for Elissa, even though she rode alone; she wore immaculately tailored jodhpurs and shirt with a tie. Rowan had the impression that the attire and not the mount was of first importance with Elissa, but she might have been doing her an injustice, for she was unquestionably an accomplished horsewoman.

She rode up to Rowan's side. 'What do you think of him?' she asked, but her tone really said, 'What do you think of me?'

'Fine.' Rowan decided that that answer would do for both of them. She asked, 'Is Nicholas satisfied with the grey?'

'He's pleased at his quick pick-up and has asked me to do this light exercising, if that's what you mean,' Elissa said with her characteristic occasional sharpness – she could be very sweet, but somewhere, Rowan felt, she carried a chip.

'I didn't mean it like that,' Rowan said, 'I just meant was Nicholas satisfied that it would soon be fit enough to rejoin the troupe.' To introduce a lighter note, Rowan laughed, 'Because when I lose Grey's visitors I lose some eating trade. The boys have promised to patronize me each time they come down.'

'But it all depended, you said, on the boss of the outfit. A – Larry, wasn't it?'

'You have a good memory.'

'Not at all, I just happened to think it was an unusual name.'

'Another form of Laurie, probably, short for Lawrence.' But Rowan spoke to nothing, for all at once Elissa had pulled on the grey's rein and cantered him off.

'I told her not to do that.' It was Nicholas now standing with Rowan. 'I told her to take him easy. She's an unpredictable girl, especially since—'

'The end of the affair?'

'Yes, Rowan. I'm afraid, apart from a settling marriage up here for her, so taking a load off my shoulders, I can't bank much on my sister's help.' He was looking wistfully at Rowan.

There was no mistaking that look, and Rowan burst out laughing.

'Nicholas, I do believe you're being nice to me with an end in view, and that end is help with your stud.'

'There could be something else as well, Rowan, there could be very easily.' Now his eyes were warm.

'Were I in Elissa's position, that position of having a brother anxious to "place" me, I would be doing very well,' Rowan said sincerely. 'Not only a vet surgeon with his own stud but an exceptionally nice man as well. But I'm not in that position, Nicholas, and I happen to be in real need of help myself, and that need just now absorbs me.

The caff' . . . she did not correct herself this time . . . 'absorbs me.'

'When it stops absorbing you, you could let me know.' But seriously, Rowan . . . yet do believe me I was serious just then . . . are you in need of assistance with Tom Thumb? Perhaps Elissa—'

'I could call on Elissa some time, and I think she would enjoy it.'

'A steady procession of men,' commented Nicholas drily, 'I know she'd enjoy it. But if it isn't help in that way then what?'

'I face opposition from my step-cousins – and I can tell you that that "step" surprised me.'

'Can you tell me more?' he asked, interested.

Glad to confide in someone, Rowan did.

She enjoyed that evening much better than the night before. Elissa had got things in place, if sketchily, and Nicholas had managed to get a timber-cutter's wife to come and help during the day in the house. The woman had left a meal that was not s. and e., and which Rowan enjoyed.

During the music that followed, the household was descended upon by the R.R., the Rough Riders. The boys had travelled down from Round Corner to see the grey, and after they had visited him they took little persuasion to stop on for drinks, coffee . . . and a dance on the wide verandah. Both Elissa and Rowan thoroughly enjoyed the heavy hopping with these young giants in boots, and they all leaned against the verandah rail afterwards laughing at the sight they must have made.

'I thought,' said Rowan when she regained her breath, 'that you could only leave the grey here if your boss O.K.'d it.'

'That's right, but he's gone.'

'Gone?' It was Elissa, sharply interested, for some

reason.

'Down to Melbourne. He'll be back and then hot-footing it no doubt, to see if the fellow is being properly looked after.'

'He comes from Melbourne?' Again it was Elissa.

'Yes. Look, the next rodeo is on Wednesday. Here's some tickets for you girls.'

'You gave me some before,' Rowan reminded him.

'They won't be current now. Take these. *And come.*'

Rowan started to say she would be unable to attend, being a business woman, but Elissa acepted the tickets for them both, and soon afterwards the lorries rattled off.

'I hope you two enjoyed your night,' complained Nicholas feelingly. '*I* never scored a dance.'

'What would you expect with fifteen males and one of them merely my brother?' laughed Elissa.

'I'm not Rowan's brother.'

'Then you weren't quick enough,' advised Elissa. 'Good night. I'm going to bed.'

She left everything as it was, so Rowan took up the used cups and glasses. Nicholas helped her, worrying because Rowan had enough of this to do all day.

'I only hope I continue to,' she sighed. 'Don't fret, Nicholas, I enjoyed tonight, too. All of it, even this washing up, it's home washing up and that's different. At least anyway it took everything out of my mind. I forgot my worries jumping around like that.'

'You should have more fun, you should avail yourself of those passes, for instance. You must get out some time.'

'I haven't been here a week yet,' she reminded him.

'But you must have time off, otherwise you'll become a dull girl.'

'Is that the doctor talking?'

'The horse doctor,' he grinned; he was very friendly

and easy.

Rowan was thinking this as she got into bed, thinking how much easier he was than her trustee. Everything was round the wrong way, she sighed; Nicholas should have been Jonathan, Jonathan Nicholas . . . though could it still have mattered with a profit clause to fulfil? She decided not to worry, and slept.

The next morning was as perfectly balmy as the previous mornings. Barney had said the only weather worries up here were the cyclones that sometimes hit the coast.

'We miss the real coastal impact,' he had said, 'but we can get some diabolical winds, at least they do diabolical things to the cane.'

'Mr. Saxby told me, he said there was a pocket of weather here that made a manual cut necessary.'

'Yes, you've no idea of the distorted shapes Jemima left us in.'

'Jemima?'

'Our last cyclone. Then Helen wasn't too kind, either. But don't worry, like the Joe Blakes they're not with us all that much.'

There was no sign of a cyclone today. The sky was a tender blue, with here and there a few blurred little pink clouds, leftovers, Rowan knew, from a narganoo sunrise . . . she smiled at herself at that . . . for she had seen the blaze of crimson through the window of her bedroom when she had first opened her eyes, and the countryside had seemed literally enfolded in flag-bright bunting.

Of course, her thoughts went idly on, red sky at morning was shepherd's warning, but here there were no sheep because of the danger of foot rot so close to the coast, Barney had told her, so there were no shepherds, only hauliers, cane cutters, pineapple growers, banana plantationers, vets. A gingerbread man.

The gingerbread man. She frowned slightly, recalling

72

Jonathan Saxby's advice to her not to send for any family records. There had been an emphasis there, she felt. Why had he advised that? Well, she was getting the records, anyway. Shirley from whatever corner it was that served their particular telephone connection had read the cable back to her, and she had seemed very reliable.

She walked slowly, not because she was unwilling to reach work, already she knew she was enjoying that work, enervating though it was, but because it was such a glorious day, or at least the morning promise of glory. There were several little houses far behind her climbing the tiers of the lower foothills that reached up eventually to those fascinating domes and minarets of the range, and standing awhile to look back she thought of the villages of Tuscany she had read about with their climbing white houses built on the sides of cobbled streets, though these little farmlets had no streets and were mostly green timber, often merging into the silver-green of the ever-present acacias until only a thread of blue woodsmoke marked their existence. She would like to go up there, she thought, and look down on the patchwork of crop colours below, further out to the dreamy islands of the Barrier Reef. It seemed impossible that Jemima, or Helen, or whatever her name was could ever sweep over those protective islands to disturb this present tender calm.

When she entered Eats, Barney told her it had been calm there, too. 'Not too calm, there's a nice little sum in the kitty, but no rush, Rowan. Which reminds me, you're to take a day off soon.'

She looked at him in inquiry. After all, this was her business. Then she remembered. It was only her business for as long as he, as Jonathan Saxby, said Yes. Undoubtedly Mr. Saxby had decreed this.

'Oh, no,' said Barney when she said so, 'there always

73

has to be a day off. Even Thommo, your Uncle Tom, had a day off.'

'Shut up shop?' asked Rowan incredulously.

'No.' A pause. 'Nancy came over.' Actually Barney went red. He was always a ruddy leather colour, but now the red crept near his ears which were not leather.

'Does Nancy like that?'

'Likes it very well,' he said offhandedly, 'she reckons it's a change from housekeeping. It's a real day off for Nance.'

'Carrying bricks?'

'Well, I suppose so in a way. But she likes it.'

'Do you have a day off, too?'

'I think of this as my day off.' Although he tried not to betray it, a wistful note came into Barney's voice.

'Oh, Barney,' said Rowan, upset. 'You do love it.'

'Nothing to stop me keeping on loving it with you running it,' said Barney stoutly. 'Now think about your day off.'

'Mr. Saxby's orders, no doubt,' said Rowan crisply.

'No doubt.' A man had entered the horror, and the height of his shadow now that the sun had reached the door made it impossible for her not to recognize the trustee.

'Good morning, Mr. Saxby,' Rowan greeted.

'Good morning, Miss Redland. Ready for a day's work?'

'Ready.' She almost added: 'Sir.'

'Will you be ready, too, for your weekly break when it comes?'

'If you say so.' – Under her breath: 'Sir.'

'I say so. All work and no play—'

'That has already been said to me by Doctor Jarvis.'

'Doctor?'

'Horse doctor.' She laughed ... but Jonathan Saxby

74

did not laugh with her.

'One day a week,' he decreed. 'At her own request Nancy comes over. No doubt it's a break from the pressure of females, for we have quite a number of them there at present.'

'Oh, yes, the harvest. How is the harvest doing?'

'The harvest is harvested. It's now being dealt with.' He looked at her a little tentatively. 'Perhaps you would care to see it on your day off.'

She could not say no, thank you, and as a matter of fact she did want to see it, but on the other hand because it was her trustee who offered it, she could not bring herself to be gracious about it.

'Some time,' she murmured.

'Why not this time?'

She moistened her lips, still unable to concede to him. 'Because,' she said in an inspiration, 'I'm going to the rodeo.'

To her surprise he did not pounce on her for that, which she rather had expected. 'You certainly must go to a rodeo,' he agreed. 'I'll see to some tickets.'

'I . . . we already have them.'

His brows raised. She told him about their visitors last night at the stud and the passes they had been given for Wednesday. She did not mention the party.

'I'm going to the Corner myself on Wednesday on business, I'll drive you,' he offered.

'There's Elissa, too.'

'That was my main reason for offering,' he proffered blandly. 'I can't see that little one sitting beside a truckie.'

'But you can see me?'

'Yes, Rowan Redland, I can see you.' He was looking narrow-eyed at her now, sly amusement in the slits.

'You mean I'm—'

75

'I mean you're not a delicate piece of porcelain,' he grinned hatefully, 'more the tough old man.'

'You're impossible!'

'And so would Elissa be in a truck. Oh, I know she'd enjoy it, she would enjoy all male company, but it can get rough and dusty up there.'

'But I could take it?'

'You're taking all this, aren't you?' He looked around him at the galvanized horror.

'If that is meant as a compliment . . .'

'As a matter of fact, it was.' He said it so seriously she decided to leave it at that.

'But what makes you think we'd get a lift?' she asked.

'Of course you'd get a lift in Queensland.' He looked at her in complete surprise at such a query.

'Nicholas might want to go, he might want us with him.'

All at once Jonathan Saxby seemed to weary of the subject.

'Watch your supplies,' he advised shortly. 'I think the steak order could be speeded up. Have a word with Barney.'

'But—' His abrupt altering of the the topic confused her, but she had no opportunity to be confused long, as a line of trucks pulled up, and when she had dealt with them all an hour later she knew that her trustee had been long gone.

She had another episode to deal with that morning. A lone truck came along around eleven o'clock, that lull time after late breakfast and before early lunch. The driver seemed only a boy, but she knew that the most stringent road rules applied here, that they would demand that he was a mature man. But in his exhausted state, he became a boy again. When Rowan asked him if he wanted the usual, he nodded, then put his head in his hands as she went out. A little concerned, several times during her cooking she peeped in at him, and he was still like that. But when she took in the finished tray, his head was right down on the table, and he was asleep.

He had no offsider. She did not know the law about that, but she rather thought there would be one regarding reliefs. She looked down on him in sympathy for a few seconds, he seemed very young, very immature, then decided to take back the tray and keep the dishes hot while he rested for a while.

Then she noticed that he was not really resting, that his hands were clenching and unclenching. A thin tear actually ran down his pale cheek. The boy . . . the *man* needed rest. Proper rest. He should lie down, not be propped up here.

She wondered if she could get him to Barney's couch, but she doubted it. For all his slenderness he was wiry, and if he resisted, as he probably would resist, for these hauliers were determined, ambitious men, she would be no match for him.

She glanced to the door, hoping for custom, hoping even for her step-cousin measuring up the land across the motorway again. But there was no one.

She thought of Nicholas. It would not take her long to run down the track. She made the young truckie as comfortable as she could with a cushion, then set off.

She was in luck. She had only got as far as the bend when she heard a car approaching. It was the vet, and he nodded as she poured out her story, left the car in the track and ran back with her.

The boy still slept, but between them they got him to Barney's couch, and here Nicholas did some horse-doctoring as he said, with a serious face now, no fun. He turned to Rowan.

'He's all right, just overdone it. He should have an offsider, but probably his excuse will be that he's picking one up further along.'

'Excuse?'

'These hauls are strictly policed, Rowan, so he would need an excuse, and rightly so, because we have a bad record with fatigue accidents. This boy is fatigued.'

'Why does he do it?'

'Why do any of them do it? Good money, and a family that needs that money. They drive themselves to a standstill. Look, he's coming out now.'

The boy had come out. He looked at them in bewilderment a moment, then in panic.

'How long have I—'

'Not long,' Rowan assured him. 'But frankly I wish it had been longer.'

'I have this time thing,' said the young driver, 'I've got to make it, or— You see, it's my first haul.'

'If you've any sense,' advised Nicholas kindly, 'it'll be your last. Oh, I know the money's good, but you have to be the right type.' He paused. 'You're not.'

'I'm a good driver.'

'I'm sure of it. But you're not tough, hard, disciplined – oh, a score of things that go to make up what this entails.'

'Betty—' murmured the boy unhappily.

'Your girl?'

'My wife.' He didn't look old enough for that.

Nicholas finished for him: 'Betty would want you alive, not asleep at the wheel and then not alive any more.'

'Black coffee will fix me.'

'With steak and eggs with it,' said Rowan firmly. Was it Rowan Redland talking, Rowan Redland of Miss Grimbell's Select Hostel who only a week ago had planned cucumber sandwiches and cinnamon toast? 'Bread and butter, tea with milk and sugar, and a wash-up. And a—'

'It does sound good,' the boy smiled a little wistfully.

Over the meal he admitted it had not been all he thought. The open road, he had dreamed, no boss driving you, no one watching you, good money at the end.

'And death at the corner,' Nicholas said.

The boy gave a little shiver. 'I did come near to it last night. I went through some miles of forest . . . you know how trees can be at night. At one time I even thought—'

'That a truck was coming at you from the wrong side of the road, so you crossed over and only crossed back in time to avoid an oncoming truck on his right side?'

'Yes,' said the driver. He said uncertainly, 'Someone told me there are pills . . .'

'No good for you,' said Nicholas. 'The only good medicine for you is to get back to Betty. It was Betty?'

'Yes.'

'And no more open road, no trucking, because that road won't open very long the way you're going.'

'I've only paid one instalment on the truck.'

'I can see that. It's virtually new. It particularly interested me because it happens to be the very make I'm after.'

Outside Rowan heard the noon lunchers arriving. She sped out. She was not as prepared as she should be. Also she had not cut any packets of corned dog and mustard pickle.

The next hour raced by, and all the time the boy and Nicholas remained cloistered together. Then at last the final Knight of the Road, for today's dinner rush, anyway, called 'B'seeing you,' and went off.

And Nicholas came out.

'He's sleeping again on the couch, after which he'll take a lift south. He won't have any trouble getting one.'

79

'But his load?'

'The first empty, or semi-empty, will be only too glad to pick it up for him. Besides a tip here there'll be the pay-off at the destination.'

'What about his truck?' Rowan asked next.

'*My* truck.'

'Oh, Nicholas, is it?'

'I wasn't being kind when I said it was the one I wanted, it *was* the one. But there was a waiting list and I knew it would be a matter of months. But as things have turned out it's not even a matter of days. A vet and a stud man must have something other than cars.'

'So you've taken it over?'

'Yes. I'm lucky, Rowan.'

'Perhaps . . . but you're still kind, you're still—'

Suddenly overwhelmed at the happy ending to it all, a boy who was not built for all this, a boy who would have turned to the pills he had spoken of, to anything to keep him on the road, now returned instead to where he should never have left, returned to his young wife, a feeling of profound relief took possession of Rowan.

On an impulse she leaned up and kissed Nicholas, kissed him fondly, gratefully. He held on to her appreciatively in return.

The shadow of a vehicle across the doorway sent Rowan withdrawing from the vet. Goodness, what if the customer had seen the little act, though these hauliers, she thought, were easygoing men.

But this one was not so easygoing. He was backing out again. Shrugging with annoyance at loss of trade, for she had not done too well today, Rowan went to the door.

It was a car, not a truck, that was speeding down the motorway. It was the trustee's.

CHAPTER FIVE

Jonathan Saxby's invitation ... though it had come more as a command than an offer ... to conduct the girls to the rodeo suited Nicholas well, because he needed his own car to take him to the nearest motor registry to fix up the truck transfer from the old to the new driver.

'It's a more complicated business than a private car,' he said. 'I never dreamed there were so many forms.'

The arrangement suited Elissa, too. She had seen Jonathan's smart roadster which he said he would be driving, and heartily approved of it— She also had met Jonathan and approved of him.

When he called round on the Wednesday morning, Elissa had taken the trouble to get down to Tom Thumb so that he would not need to go up the track, and Rowan soon saw why ... and smiled. Directly the car stopped, Elissa put herself near the driver. That, thought Rowan with amusement, would be typically Elissa.

She looked lovely in a lemon slacksuit that suited her fair hair and complimented her slender figure. Rowan felt she herself looked drab in comparison, but she had got to the caff an hour earlier so as to lighten the day's work for the others by doing some sandwich preparation, and had not dared wear anything pale. She only hoped her simple deep blue linen did not appear too workaday.

Nancy had scolded her for the preparation. 'What do you think I come here for?' she demanded.

About to answer, 'I don't know, Nancy, what do you come here for?' Rowan had stopped herself. She had caught a fleeting look between the housekeeper and Barney. Into the pleasant tanned face of which Nancy had said the freckles had joined together had crept a pretty pink. Why, thought Rowan, I do believe that pair—

She had had no opportunity to finish her thoughts, though, for Jonathan had pulled up, got out and they had got in.

They had set out for the day's excitement.

To Rowan, it seemed a long way to go for a rodeo, but up here she knew distance was considered a mere detail. Elissa, in the middle, said it was longer than Victorians usually went, and laughed cosily when Jonathan then asked her slyly how far did Victorians go. On the outside, Rowan only half listened to their playful repartee; the scenery was absorbing her.

Never had she seen such quick changes, such variations. First it was cane, mile after mile of gracefully waving, damply shining green, making a patchwork quilt where the plantings were in varying stages of growth. At times narrow-gauge railways ... called tramways ... broke up the mosaic, and little laden waggons puffed along with their load.

'It's good cane,' Jonathan said proudly, 'rises fourteen feet in parts, though, of course, about four feet of that is "top". Other places beat us in height, but we have the biggest sugar content.' He glanced teasingly down at Elissa. 'All that for sugar for your tea!'

She smiled coquettishly back at him, but Rowan felt that she always did this, just as she took the seat near the man; it simply was Elissa. She acted all the time. When Jonathan described the beasties that came out of the cane, the mice, sugar 'roaches, toads who sat at six inches, she gave a feminine little squeal and implored him not to let her out.

'You'll be all right, we're among the nuts now.'

These were the Macadamia nuts, and where they grew

you would also find a belt of rain forest, the trustee said. The nuts were picked up from the ground beneath the trees, the harvesting wasn't any trouble, but the cracking for the kernels was, for the shells were iron hard. But science was overcoming that now. They had been going through softwood country, planted timber, for it also needed the rain, and Rowan caught her breath at the sight of the regulated softwood trees rising hundreds of clean straight feet. At the edge of the plantings the unregulated ones rose, too, festooned in parasitic fig and occasionally trailing orchid.

They stopped for pineapple drinks at a pineapple plantation, then Jonathan took a mountain detour so that the girls could look down, really look down, on the embroidery of the Barrier Reef islands, paisley patterned from this height in greens and blues, yellows and greys.

At last what Rowan had waited for, and seriously wondered if Queensland really possessed, loomed up. Her first town.

'Not huge,' said Jonathan, 'like Townsville, Bundaberg, some others, nor by English' . . . he smiled sylyly . . . 'or *Victorian* standards, but we at Cosy Corner think Round Corner's a big smoke.'

It was sprawling, comfortable, planted with bauhinia and jacaranda, and today had a sense of expectancy. 'It's time,' explained Jonathan, 'for the procession to go by.'

'A procession, too?'

'Well, not exactly, but all these Gold Cup rodeos open up with a Cobb and Co. display down the main street.'

They watched the parade, then Jonathan said he had seen enough rodeos to suit him and would pick them up in the afternoon. After Elissa's cosiness during the trip, Rowan had rather expected that the girl would prefer to forgo the rodeo and stay with Jonathan, but something had come over Elissa, she was so eager to go in that she

83

barely gave Jonathan a farewell wave.

'Oh, do hurry, Rowan,' she complained.

There were crowds milling into the enclosure, but the boys had reserved their seats. Nothing had started as yet, but it was the same scene as at all such outdoor gatherings, the same food tents, drink tents, commercial merry-go-rounds, hooplas, chocolate wheels and shies, all their attendants eager to snare the before-rodeo trade. Everywhere except inside the big corral the grass was already being worn thin from passing feet, and becoming littered with lolly wrappers and butts.

Behind the corral in stalls the riders and their offsiders waited, the riders resplendent in ten-gallon hats and brightly checked shirts. Also, whispered Elissa to Rowan, the mounts waited. She looked pale and a little nervous, and Rowan asked her was there anything wrong.

'Of course not. Why should there be?'

'No reason, only you seemed—'

'Well, it's all silly, isn't it? I mean—'

'What do you mean, Elissa?'

'It would be dangerous,' Elissa said, and she sounded wretched.

'These men know what they're about.'

'What if a man – doesn't?'

'Then he wouldn't go in for such a thing.'

'He – might,' Elissa said in a low tone.

There was no time to pursue that subject, for a buzz of excitement had risen to a high pitch, and to hear anything one would have had to ask the speaker to shout. The show had begun.

Rowan enjoyed it completely. She watched the strong boomerang legs of the competitors as they sat long in the saddle, she caught her breath at men on foot in the arena making split-second leaps for the surrounding rails as a horse thundered towards them. The horsemanship, roping, drafting and roughriding kept her fascinated, the risking of necks and limbs for the honour of being the champion.

Several times she heard Elissa breathing tightly beside her, but she could not take her eyes off the virile scene, the tough, hard-riding, lean, tanned, leggy men, the swirl of flying hooves as a fresh four-legged candidate who hadn't been ridden in months took his turn in humiliating his burden into the dust as he pig-rooted, kicked and threw made her forget all about Elissa.

Only when the lunch break came did she remember her. Elissa was gone.

So the girl was not so tough as she liked you to think, mused Rowan ... though tough was not the right word, tough, according to the trustee, was for her. She was not so blasé, Rowan thought instead. Either that, or she had decided that Jonathan was a better day's sport. Somehow she did not think so, though; for all her coquetry on the journey up Rowan had had the impression that Elissa was not really interested, that she had something else on her mind.

She wondered where to look for her. Certainly at none of the food or drink tents, they would not be Elissa's choice. Perhaps, she thought, not adverse to the idea herself after a week of steak and eggs, some dainty tea shop fare in the town. She left the arena.

The main street was deserted. She supposed it was a public holiday and that all the shops would be closed, in which case she had better eat at the rodeo after all. She turned to go back.

'Had enough already?' It was the trustee, and he was coming down the steps of a hotel.

'Not really. I enjoyed it tremendously. But either Elissa didn't or she saw something – or somebody. Anyway, she wasn't there when I looked round.'

85

'You must have been absorbed,' he laughed. 'Come in and I'll buy you a drink.'

'Tea would go better.'

'I think I can manage that, too.'

'But Elissa—'

'Don't worry, let her do that.'

'I can't – I mean, after all, she came with us. Also' . . . stubbornly . . . 'she's younger than I am.'

'And you're very old.' While he was talking he was guiding Rowan to a table. He asked the waitress for tea . . . a pause . . . and cucumber sandwiches. He did not look at Rowan when he said it, but when eventually he did look, he grinned. For a moment Rowan looked sternly back at him, then she laughed as well.

It was pleasant to be civilized again. That was not the right word, but it was the general meaning. The china was thin, the bread was thin, the cucumbers thin.

'A bit different,' insinuated Jonathan, 'from doorstops and mustard pickle.'

Rowan murmured uneasily that Elissa would have appreciated this. 'I do feel awful not knowing she left.'

'Then perish the thought. She didn't want you to know.'

'What?'

'That's true. I met one of the riders . . . incidentally they've done their stint for today . . . and he gave me a message not to wait for our lady.'

'But we can't do that, we can't not wait,' she protested.

'Why not? She's adult, she knows her own mind.'

'She can't stay with those men.'

'They didn't say she was, all that was mentioned was that she asked to look around their caravans. Probably she's finding her own way home with Nicholas.'

'Oh, yes,' Rowan remembered, 'he had to come up to

deal with some registration detail. But Elissa wouldn't know where to find him.'

'The boys will take her. Look' ... after a pause ... 'our Elissa isn't about to be eaten. Now eat your last sandwich, and decide what *you* are going to do.'

'What do you mean?'

'Are you going to attend this afternoon's session, or are you coming home with me?'

'I suppose it would be a break for Barney and Nancy if I—'

'I said home. My home.'

'I'm not going there!' Rowan exclaimed.

'Why not? You go to the stud every night.'

'But that's my board, I mean it's where I sleep.'

'You slept once at Narganoo.'

'I know, but—'

She did not finish. He sat silent. But presently he said, 'Well, I'm going home. If you want to see the rodeo out you'll have to find your own way back.'

She stared at him indignantly. 'You invited me to come!'

'Do you recall me inviting you to return?'

'No, but I naturally assumed—'

'Look, I don't want to be unreasonable, but I have a lot to do at Narganoo, and you've surely seen your fill at this morning's session, particularly when the only ones you've been interested in are now over.'

'I know that, and I have seen enough, but—'

'Yes, Miss Redland?'

'I still can't see why you can't return me to Tom Thumb. After all, if one invited someone then presumably—'

'You haven't let me finish. I will, of course, take you back to the café ... *in time*. But surely if you can put in all day at Eats, all night at the Jarvises, you can spare a

87

few minutes en route at Narganoo.'

'If you'd said that in the beginning I wouldn't be arguing now,' she sighed.

'Then you're ready to come?'

'Yes.' All the same when they reached the street, she looked around her, wishing she could see Elissa.

'I assure you she's all right, those boys are all right.' A pause. 'I don't know if you've noticed anything with our lady, but to my idea she gives the definite impression of needing to find out something.'

'Find out what?'

He shrugged. 'We all have to find out something.'

'Like I have to find out the family chart.'

He turned on her sharply at that. 'You're not still on that idea?'

'Why not? It's my family.'

He calmed down, though she could see it took an effort. 'I agree that finding out that your mother's sisters and brother were only the step varieties, your cousins the same, was a shock, but surely you don't have to check up.'

'What does it matter if I do?'

He had reached the parked roadster and he opened the door for her. He did not answer her question.

They retraced their way, but without detours this time, no stopping to look at the undulating cane, to gaze down at an embroidery of islands. In much less time than they had taken to go up, he was leaving the road before the restaurant to turn in at that arched Narganoo.

Though she would not have admitted it to him, she found herself eager to see the place by daylight. It had been daylight when he had driven her to the café that first morning, but she had run to his sounding of the horn, not wanting to give him any cause for complaint. Now it was different. She had time to look around.

By colonial standards, she thought, it would be considered an old house, and that could be true, for he had said that his grandparents had lived here. On the cement platform beneath the piles on which it stood were collections of beautiful ferns, the delicate water ones, the more robust fireplants and crotons. Travellers' palms, frangipanni in both pink and white and scarlet hibiscus dotted the lawns.

He got out and led the way in to the wide hall.

'Do you want to wait here while I go across to the factory or would you like to come?'

'You're not ordering me now?'

He looked at her thoughtfully a moment, then he crossed and took her arm.

'Come along,' he said, and whether it was order or invitation, she did not know.

The factory was next door, but reached through an elevated companionway, and it was really more bungalow than factory, it was so pleasantly laid out.

It was not working. Even harvest workers, it seemed, had their day off, and today was a district holiday. He took Rowan over the different stages of the ginger, explaining it by a large coloured legend on the wall, placed there for the city cutters, he said, who did not know a stem from a root. – 'That is, when they arrive,' he added with an edged smile.

'The big boss?'

'They take it from me, I don't browbeat them like I do you.'

'Do you?'

'I think you think I do.' He left the legend, and showed her the slicing and pulping machinery that came after the manual peeling. She was fascinated with it, with the ingenious method of it. She asked him had he designed the machinery himself, and he said deprecatingly, 'I think it has evolved more than been designed. We all had a hand, my grandfather, my father, then I did.' She noticed, as before, there was a slight hesitancy as he spoke of his relations.

She saw the different bottles for the different products, the attractive labels, the cane gift baskets which particularly appealed to her, then turned to see that he had made tea.

'Canteen variety, but I can recommend it. You always have to look after employees with a good cup. Also' . . . producing nutty brown bread which he had spread with butter . . . 'good ginger products. This is a new product our chemist has been evolving.'

It was delicious, totally different from the ginger marmalade, more a ginger nut paste. As he watched her sampling it, she saw him add liquid ginger to his own tea. 'You *are* a ginger man,' she said with a laugh.

'You mean red and hot?' He put the cup down.

This was the kind of light talk he and Elissa had used between them on the way up. Rowan did not respond.

At first she thought he was not going to continue the subject, then he drawled, 'So it's all right then for a vet, but not for that ginger man, as you call me.'

'I only say that in fun.'

He was silent for a moment . . . but waitingly silent. 'And the *other*, was it fun, too?'

'What are you talking about, and what do you mean is it all right for Nicholas?'

'The tender treatment,' he said directly, 'as opposed to the six-foot pole treatment, six-foot pole between the two of us, with which you allot me.'

'I don't understand you.'

'Then I understood that kiss. And yet in a way I didn't, for it seemed to be you who was kissing, and isn't it the lady's prerogative to be the kissed?'

She had gone a dull red. 'I can explain that.'

'Never explain a kiss.'

'All the same, it will be explained.' Not giving him time to intervene, she quickly told the story of the young truckie.

'Yes, there are occasions when you get them like that, a haulier has to be born for the job, just as a painter or a writer. He has to have the stamina, the right attitude, the staying power – but good heavens, woman, why call on Nicholas Jarvis?'

'He – well, he's a—'

'A horse doctor. You've said so yourself. I'm not decrying his ability, far from it, but why run up to the house—'

'I didn't have to run that far.'

'When two steps' ... he ignored her ... 'to the phone would have got me.'

She was angry with herself because she knew now that that was what she should have done. He was the trustee, she depended on him. Yet in a matter of emergency she had turned somewhere else.

'I never thought of you,' she admitted.

'Yet you thought of Jarvis?'

'Yes.'

'Because what you rewarded him with you had experienced before?'

'What is this? An inquisition?' she demanded crossly.

'Just a question, Miss Redland. I'm here to see if you can carry on where your uncle left off, or' ... a deliberate pause ... 'if you just carry on.'

He was being abominable, intentionally so. Leaning across, hardly aware of what she was doing, she raised an angry arm.

She didn't connect with his cheek, though, he caught

the arm before she could do so, and whirling her around, he kissed her instead— Only there was not the least doubt who was the kissed now, who the one who kissed.

'Well,' he said when he had finished, 'how many points ... you're keen on points, aren't you? ... for the ginger man?'

They left at once. Even though Rowan hurried out, he was in the car before her. She scrambled after him, and they drove without conversation to Tom Thumb.

Nancy was ready to drive home, but Barney stayed on. He asked Rowan about the rodeo, but did not seem anxious for her reply. He seemed depressed, and Rowan knew why. This place had been his dream, and the dream was gone.

They were both a little glad when the rodeo boys turned up to look in on the grey, and to eat while they were here.

They had Elissa with them, for she had not returned with Nicholas after all, which should have relieved Rowan ... if she had been capable of relief. She was not.

She was glad Elissa was back, though, even though there was something different about her, an excitement, a tension. A nervousness you could not put a finger on, but was still there. She must remember to tell Nicholas to keep an eye on his sister.

Her mind baulked sharply at that. Ask *Nicholas*? What had Jonathan Saxby just said of Nicholas? The tender treatment. But she hadn't ... she hadn't. He was hateful to suggest such a thing.

But more hateful still that punishing kiss, for that was what it had been and what it was meant for, punishment, because he was the trustee, the final word, the judge, because he had, or considered he had, that right.

'Rowan, you're red, are you feverish?' It was Elissa,

92

still looking ... to Rowan, anyway ... a different Elissa.

'No. Mr. Saxby gave me some ginger, it must have been very hot.'

Red and hot. He had said that, too. He was the most objectionable, impossible man she had ever encountered.

And he was the trustee.

CHAPTER SIX

THE next morning Nicholas took delivery of a small bunch of horses he had personally selected before he came north, and on which he intended to build his future stud.

The ponies had left Victoria when he and Elissa had, but on his instructions their journey had been leisurely, no time clause imposed. If any of the consignment showed the least strain of travel, the journey was to be stopped and a break made until the animal was fit again. As it happened, the vet told Rowan, the trip up had gone famously. Upon arrival in their padded boxes, Nicholas had gone over every animal very closely. He was delighted that they had arrived in such excellent condition.

'Now is the testing time,' he said, 'now I will be testing my theory that this sub-tropical climate will avail them all that they got in the more stimulating south. I can't see why not. The air is soft here, but there's no rule I know of that there must be a sharp edge. The important thing is the rain, that there's a good but smooth fall, and not the deluge variety as further up the coast.'

'What about cyclones?'

'They're infrequent, also back here they shouldn't affect us, Rowan. We're very sheltered.' He smiled happily. 'I feel I'm going to do well.'

He was so boyishly lit up, Rowan could not help being enthusiastic with him. She went eagerly round the boxes he had had prepared, modern, commodious enclosures, a special section for foaling. 'Though in these latitudes,' Nicholas said, 'I've no doubt foaling can be done outside, something that the mare vastly prefers.'

He had provided the area, though, and done it with a view to the mother's peace of mind as well as vet needs. It was cheerful, bright, even providing a window for the mother's benefit, and much larger than usual.

'Why not?' Nicholas asked.

'Why not?' agreed Rowan, impressed with the storage compartment, the saddle horse, the provision for girths, stirrup leathers, buckleguards. There were plenty of benches, a handy number of hooks, a place for brushes, cloths, wither pads. Everything had been thought of, even a record book and a calendar . . . 'Must have a calendar,' Nicholas smiled.

'It's perfect, Nicholas.'

'I'm hoping it will be. Now come and meet the boys and girls.'

They were a fine troupe, a few specials from New Zealand which provided the cream, though would the cream persist when the warm air of Queensland took over from the apple breath of that south island across the Tasman?

'We'll see,' said Nicholas. 'Here is Bright Bruce, here is Golden Haze. Meet Captain, Smart Girl, Westbound and' . . . a pause . . . 'Miss Mary.'

'There was a note in your voice just then,' smiled Rowan. 'I think the beautiful box is for Miss Mary. I think Miss Mary should be Mrs. Mary.'

'Mrs. Captain actually, for she's the Captain's lady. Yes, Rowan, Miss Mary will be my first effort.'

'How is she doing?'

'Splendidly. She took the journey with no trouble. I really feel something special with Miss Mary.'

'The firstborn,' smiled Rowan. She added, 'Nicholas, I'm happy for you.'

'I'm happy for myself, but happiness has to include others. Elissa. – You. I only wish my happiness could be yours, Rowan. I mean *actually* yours. I know it's early to speak yet, I'm not established, and you've not made up your mind, but—'

'What do you mean, not made up my mind? I have. I want to make my venture a success.'

'I have the feeling you say that, but that it's not all that important. I mean not like the stud is to me.'

'I suppose that can only be expected. You're dealing with flesh, I'm dealing with – well, things to make flesh. Steak. Eggs. It's entirely different, Nicholas.'

'That wasn't exactly what I meant. I always feel somehow with you that you're – well, waiting, kind of filling in time, until – well, until something . . . *someone* happens. Rowan, I'd like to be around then.'

'You're quite wrong,' she laughed, 'but thanks, anyway, in all your turmoil of work for even thinking of me. I love your troupe, Nicholas, and I'll be down to look at them every moment I'm not running in and out with laden trays.' She smiled at him, then hurried off, for already she was five minutes past her usual time for relieving Barney.

It was not until mid-morning that it came ominously to Rowan that she might not be running in and out much longer with laden trays. While she had been occupied with a procession of new cars being transported north on a series of large haulage trucks, something had happened across the road. Actually a prefabricated building had arrived, and even at this moment was being eased on to its piers.

So the opposition had begun!

She looked at it with hate . . . she would have been surprised with how much hate. She had not expected quite so nice a building, though she supposed it was the freshness of it compared to the dinginess of the horror that really affronted her. Even as she stood, her step-cousin turned round and waved his arm, then indicated the very artistic sign that was to be erected: 'The Out-look'. Then: 'Breakfasts. Dinners. Teas'. There was not, she saw bitterly, any 'Eats'.

She went back into the kitchen and sat down at the table for a while. She had known it was to come, but now that it had she felt enraged. How could anyone be so mean? Oh, she knew that everyone had a right to open shop, just as Uncle Tom had opened shop in his turn, but this went further than that, these step-cousins of hers were only doing this for spite, spite because the child of the unconnected child of the family had been left the spoils. If somewhere inside her she agreed with their resentment . . . and Rowan in all fairness did . . . she would not now admit it. She spent a few moments actually crying with childish rage.

Then she got up and looked around, knowing once more all the horror she had known the first day she had come here. No wonder a decent place was opening across the road! Well, she might as well shut shop, for no one, simply no one, would pass that clean roof to come here. She felt like going outside and putting a match to Tom Thumb.

The mood passed as soon as it had come. Rowan had always been a fighter, even though, as one of the Grimbell girls had said of their cafeteria struggles and Rowan's unlucky results: 'If there's one stale sandwich or one dud cake, Rowan will get it.' That brought back the memory of old lunch ordeals, the sheer joy she had known when she had learned of her inheritance. A little tea shop, she had thought, cucumber sandwiches, light music, an elf with a peaked cap above the name Tom Thumb, not – not Eats.

All at once she hated that Eats, and plotted against it. It didn't matter about the smaller T. Thumb, that could remain, if only ... wickedly ... to annoy the Thumbs who had *not* inherited from Uncle T. But Eats must come down. Marching to the back of the house, she took up a ladder she had noticed before and brought it round to the sign. There she mounted it and began to push and pull. The sign offended her. If she was to compete with The Outlook across the road, with Breakfast, Dinners, Teas, she would make this her first move. She forced it up, then she forced it down. And the next minute she was down – on the ground. The sign was scattered around her, for each of the letters was separate. The T. Thumb, though, beneath them, that must have been connected with Eats, had descended intact.

It was there, on the strip of cement, that Jonathan found her, and he ran forward to see if she was hurt. She was quite conscious, if absolutely furious she had not got herself up again before he could find her, anyone find her, but there was a reason. She couldn't move her foot. Her stupid impulse or at least the carrying out of her impulse, had resulted in a sprained ankle – or something like that, anyway. All she knew was she would not be able to put her foot to the ground.

'Are you all right?' Jonathan Saxby, the trustee, was bending over her.

'Yes.'

'Then what in tarnation are you doing down there? Ah ... I see!' He was looking at T. Thumb, and his face was livid with anger. 'So you wanted that down.'

'Well, it doesn't apply now, does it? Tom Thumb? I'm Redland.'

She waited for him to say, 'That's for me to decide.'

He didn't. Instead he said, 'You didn't want the name Thumb, did you, yet I would have given the best years of my life for such a name. He was one of the finest men I ever met.'

98

She looked at him in complete surprise from where she still lay. Why would he want a different name? He must have felt her surprise, for he said gruffly, 'All right, get up.'

'I can't.'

'Why? You look all right to me.'

'I don't think my ankle is, it's . . . it's sort of numb.'

'Is that why you're still down there? Why didn't you say so?' He bent down, picked her up and took her in to the couch. 'Now let me see.'

To see, he had to remove her shoe, then the long white knee-high sock she always wore instead of stockings up here, and she felt very small and stupid.

'Yes,' he said after some probing which she succeeded in not flinching over, ' a sprain. And all that to take down your uncle's name.'

'It wasn't really, it was to take down Eats. I mean haven't you seen across the road? Breakfasts, Dinners, T-teas.' At the teas the tears began to fall. Teas. Ladies in white gloves. Soft music. Fresh young girls in green pin-afores. A *nice* place.

He had left her a moment to look across the road. Now he came back. 'I'll have to get you to the hospital to have that ankle attended,' was all he said.

'It doesn't matter.'

'If by that you mean you intend calling in the horse doctor, just say it, Miss Redland.'

'I don't intend calling in Nicholas.'

'All right, we go to hospital.'

'I can't. The shop . . .'

'It'll have to be closed. Barney is at work until tonight and I can't spare Nancy.'

'I can't close it, I mean that's what the opposition is waiting for.'

'What's this you're giving me now? Up to a moment

ago you'd all but given in, you were in despair, now you're fighting back.'

'I was fighting back all along, you fool, I only wanted to remove Eats. Eats are awful.'

'*Is* awful. It's one sign.'

'It's a lot of plates of steak and eggs, so it's plural to me. And I meant ... well, I'm sure Uncle Tom wouldn't have minded that removal, anyway. What are you doing, Mr. Saxby? Mr. Saxby, I can't go. Mr. Saxby, the trucks will be along any moment. Mr. Saxby! Jonathan!'

For the trustee was carrying Rowan to the car.

They went to a nearer town than the rodeo scene this time, and in the cottage hospital Rowan was X-rayed, then suitably bound.

'No climbing ladders for you for a few weeks,' the doctor smiled.

All the way back from the hospital, Rowan kept worrying as to how she would manage when she got to Tom Thumb. How could she hope to cope with the noon rush of the s. and e.'s, the preparation of the corn and mustard pickles when she had only one foot on which to move around? She looked at Jonathan several times, silently hating him for his bland non-participation in her cares, for his attention appeared to be only on the motorway, but when he turned in at Narganoo instead of continuing along the bitumen, her silence broke, and she said sharply, 'Where are we going?'

'Where would you think?'

'Turn round at once!' she demanded.

'Along this narrow track? I'd run into the ginger rows.'

'I wish you would, I wish—'

'Yes, Miss Redland?'

'I wish,' said Rowan in a humble voice, and it cost her a lot, 'you would either reverse back or go to the house, turn round, then take me to the caff.' Annoyed at herself, especially when she heard his low throaty laugh, she corrected, 'The café.'

'The latter will be done,' he promised. Then he added casually, 'In time.' He also explained, 'Reversing along that winding track would be quite a challenge.'

She ignored the explanation. She said, 'What do you mean "in time"?'

'I meant in time. Until the swelling goes down you're staying here.'

'I'm doing nothing of the sort!'

'Then how do you propose to take yourself off? It's a long way to hop.'

'Why are you doing this?'

'As a gesture to you, you didn't think it was for myself?'

'I didn't think anything except the business, and what's going to happen. Now, of all times, when the opposition is getting ready, I must be on the spot.'

'To climb another ladder and break an arm this time?'

'I wouldn't. It was bad luck I had the accident then. Please, Mr. Saxby, go back.'

For a moment she thought he was going to concede, for he stopped the car, but she soon found out it was only to drive home a point.

'Look, what good would you be there?'

'I could hobble.'

'And mess everyone else up as you did, make the position much worse.'

'There's no one else to mess up, Barney never comes on till evening, so how could the position be worse?'

'I'm trying to be patient with you,' he said in a dangerously level voice. 'Don't try me too much. When the swelling has gone down a little, you *can* go to the café, at least you could sit and butter the bread, but until then you would be a damn nuisance. Now be a sensible girl and admit that fact.'

'I wouldn't be. Oh, can't you see I can't be?'

'You'd be so anxious you'd have the place in an uproar. Sorry, Miss Redland, you have to rest.'

'Can't it be on Barney's couch?'

'I hadn't finished. I was going to say "rest on a bed".'

She said desperately, 'Does it have to be your bed?'

He raised his brows at her choice of words, and red and discomfited, she flung, 'You know what I mean.'

'Yes. You mean the horse doctor's bed. – Now don't go trying that face-slapping any more, or I might slap back. I reckon that's the basic trouble with you, you were never slapped enough.'

'This is getting us nowhere.'

'I agree.' He started the car again.

'Why can't I . . .' she tried once more, but he paid no attention; he drove on to the house. Here, he put his finger on the horn, and, as before, Nancy came running out. At once she dissolved into sympathetic 'Oohs' and 'Ahs' and 'Poor dear' and 'Never mind, we'll have you up and around again,' and before Rowan could protest once more, she was put into bed.

It was the same room as the first night, the room with the window looking out on the ginger crop, the room that entrapped the pungency that was released when the northern sun beat down on the crimson ginger shoots. It was a completely satisfying smell, a completely satisfying view, and Rowan knew as she lay there that this smell and this view . . . and this corner of the world . . . had won her heart, she wanted to live all her life here, but how could she when even at this minute truckies were passing Eats, because Eats had closed up shop and to remain in a place like this you had to have the means.

Two tears coursed down her cheeks.

Nancy had finished making her comfortable and had fussed out to brew tea, so the voice that said, 'Is it hurting, then?' was Jonathan's. He had come silently into the room.

'No-no, b-but—'

'Make up your mind.'

'You know what the trouble is,' she said in a burst.

'Tom Thumb?'

'Yes.'

'Then be of good cheer, you have an assistant.'

'Nancy?'

'She's required here to look after you. No, Elissa.'

'Elissa?' she gasped.

'You can't be surprised. Serving bunches of males would be right up Elissa's alley.'

'Oh, yes, she'd like that, but the preparation—'

'I don't believe the girl is as feather-headed as we think. Anyway, not to worry, besides Elissa I've secured the services of a timber cutter's wife – the one, I believe, who helps at the stud now. Elissa suggested it, she said she was sure Mrs. White would be glad of the extra money.'

'Money!' echoed Rowan bleakly.

'Another not-to-worry. It will all be overcome. The only thing now is for you to un-swell, and you won't do that unless you lie and rest.'

'I could still have done that at home.'

He looked at her sharply. 'Home? Where is home?'

'Nowhere. What I meant was—'

'You meant the vet's?'

Rowan said, 'Yes.' Yet she hadn't meant it that way.

She could see he was angry. He crossed to the window and looked out for quite a long time. She felt sure he was as hot as his hot variety of ginger. At last he turned back.

'With Elissa working at the shop, you would be an imposition at the stud. Also' ... a pause ... 'you would be alone there.'

'You really mean alone with Nicholas. You really mean that this is still a formal state.'

'You said it,' he said drily. 'Now can we change the subject, please?'

'Before we do,' she said pitifully, 'is this ... my ankle, I mean ... a bad point on the judgment sheet?'

'Only if you try to fight it.'

'How long must I lie up?'

'I told you, until the swelling goes down.'

'Then can I go and help?'

'Then,' he promised, 'I'll fix a crutch for you, convey you there every morning, pick you up every night.' He added finally, 'No points lost.'

She said a little wearily, 'Not that it matters, does it. The final decision is on the profit and loss.'

'But ah,' he reminded her, 'you could both be a dead heat, and then no points lost could make you the winner.'

'I don't know why Uncle Thomas ever made such a will,' she fretted, and Jonathan Saxby said, 'I don't, either, though it was better than the first.'

'The first? Then there was another will?'

Jonathan didn't answer. He said, 'Here's tea,' and got up to help Nancy.

He did not bring up the will subject again, and something about him warned Rowan not to, either. They did not even discuss Eats.

He went out and brought in a radio player. 'What's your choice?' he asked.

'Grieg.'

'Fir trees in a land of gum?'

'And wattle, jacaranda, flame—'

'You know what,' he broke in, 'I think you like this place.'

'Little use, is it?' For a moment she forgot their unspoken pact to let the matter rest.

'There are other ways of stopping here,' he said offhandedly.

'Like?'

'Well – marrying the vet.' As she flushed, he said keenly, 'Has he asked you?' She did not answer. 'Has he?'

'Not in so many words.'

They were silent to the end of the record, then he got up and spun 'On the Trail'.

'I think that's more in keeping.'

They went to many parts of the world, but when the trustee played 'London Suite', Rowan turned her head to the wall. All at once she felt every inch of the heaven-knows-how-many inches back to England.

She was aware, though so lightly it was barely awareness, of lips on her brow. 'Sleep, little one,' Jonathan said.

He brought good reports of the café the next day, so Rowan, accepting her fate, relaxed ... and even enjoyed herself. There was no doubt that it was a comfortable house in which to nurse an ankle. Between the ginger activities, which the ginger boss said were diminishing now, Jonathan came and played records, or played Scrabble. Or sometimes just talked.

Once Rowan accepted the fact that he would not talk shop, so it was no use her trying, she enjoyed the talks. He knew this country intimately, he knew every aspect, and he had the gift of telling facts in an arresting, almost fiction-vivid manner.

She learned about cane, and how ... like the ginger

that did more than fill pretty jars for Christmas presents ... sugar did more than sweeten tea. 'Rum, power alcohol, industrial acids, vitamins and sulpha drugs,' he said.

He told her of the manual cut which they had to use here, of black-singleted men working several abreast, making deep swathes to and fro across the field, leaving the cane lying crosswise to the direction of the cut.

But it was when he spoke of the islands that his eyes gleamed. As with all Queenslanders she could see that the Barrier Reef was his joy and pride.

'It's breathtaking,' he said. 'Everywhere there are islands, hundreds of islands, islands with pine-clad cliffs rising steeply up, islands with fiord-like inlets and islands made for romantic movies with gently shelving beaches and white sands.' Suddenly aware of his enthusiasm, he said a little gruffly, 'You'll have to come.'

His enthusiasm had reached her, and she said eagerly, 'Oh, yes!'

It was not until the next morning when he arrived behind Nancy with the breakfast tray and said, 'In half an hour?' that she realized he had taken her seriously.

'But – You do mean the islands?'

'Of course. What else?'

'But how could I? I'm not on my feet.'

'You don't have to be. I'll carry you to the car, take you down to the jetty and put you in the boat. We'll only do an inner island. The joys of the outer reef are only for the sound of foot.'

It was alluring. She found suddenly she wanted to go quite desperately. But it wasn't practicable, of course. She opened her mouth to say so, but by this time he had gone.

'You'll be all right, darling,' Nancy assured her.

After the meal, Nancy got her up and helped her dress,

and exactly in the thirty minutes Jonathan came in, picked her up and carried her to the car.

'If I had a stick—' Rowan began.

'What do you think we're going for? A hoop pine crook is the very latest in crutches this season.'

He could be charming when he put himself out to be, and he did that today. While he told her tall Queensland stories – for, he said, all Queensland stories had to be tall because it was the tall state – he drove the car carefully down the steep descent to the sea, then along a stretch of coast to where his boat was bobbing up and down at the end of a small pier.

'Where we're going, of course, is only the lower end of the Reef, and the island will be within the inner Reef, but you'll get the idea.'

He put her in the small neat boat, surrounded her with the cushions Nancy had supplied, started the engine, and they pushed off.

She looked over the side at the cornflower blue water, yet for all its colour as clear as glass so that you could see the fine white sand underneath.

'Coral sand. All these beaches are. The living coral is the home of the tiny coral polyp that has built up the reef with its lime, and the beaches are the result of millions of pounding years from the sea.'

Rowan cried out with delight when a giant turtle nosed up to the surface, then lazily nosed away again.

They passed a little atoll that he said was yet another Island of a Million Birds. When she raised her brows at that, he explained, 'Right up the Reef someone will show you the Island of a Million Birds. The birds are noddy tern, and probably two million if you could count them. Look over now and you'll see the coral.'

She did, gazing at the starlike flowers, branches and mushroom formation. The clear water made it all look so close, she put out her hand.

'I wouldn't,' Jonathan advised, 'it would probably break. The saying is it breaks as easily as a heart.' He had cut the engine and was looking directly at her.

A little disconcerted, Rowan said, 'I thought we were coming for my crook.'

'We have come, if you look over your shoulder.'

She looked and saw they had reached a pine-clad island with a gentle sandy shelf, ideal for beaching a boat. A few yards more, and he jumped out and pushed the boat in.

It must have been an island Jonathan knew intimately, for he carried her unerringly to a shady palm, disappeared for a short while to return with a billy of clear water. 'This is one of the lucky isles,' he told her, 'most of them have no streams.'

Then he took sling, gun, goggles, mask and flippers out of the boat, stripped off to a wet suit he wore, and walked into the water.

'Are crutches found in the sea in these parts?' Rowan called.

'No, but lunch is. 'And' ... before he went under ... 'it won't be s. and e.'

It was snapper. Thirteen inches, three pounds of it. He said it should allay starvation till they got back again, and scaled and filleted it. He found a fireplace of stones left from his last visit, and soon the fish was cooking. Nancy had packed bread and butter and salt, and that was all that was needed.

'This is perfect,' Rowan sighed. She put her head to one side to listen to the gentle wash of the water on the reef.

'Is it as musical as trucks pulling up?' he laughed. 'As money dropping in the till?'

'Much more ... only to enjoy this there has to be those

other sounds, hasn't there?'

'Not if you're a beachcomber.'

'I'm not one. I don't think I've ever known one.'

'. . . I have,' he said tightly. A little cloud seemed to come over him.

After that, the magic seemed to go. Rowan could not have put a finger on it, said why, but something left them. Jonathan got up, climbed the hill and cut a smooth hoop pine crook. When he came back he said a little abruptly that they had better leave.

'One thing,' she remarked more for conversation, for she did not understand . . . nor like . . . the atmosphere that had crept in, 'there would be no fears on this millpond.'

'Perish that thought,' he flung. 'This millpond can blow up to a sea that can make even the most seasoned mariner blanch. Especially when Jemima strikes.'

'Oh, Jemima,' she said with contempt. 'It's a wonder one of my step-cousins didn't receive that name. Perhaps she did as a second thought. I must look when the record comes.'

He had the engine ticking quietly over, and he turned round on her. She saw that his eyes were angry slits.

'You're not on that again? Not on that damn family history?'

She looked at him in surprise. She had been surprised before at his antagonism over this subject, but now she saw he was really furious.

'Of all the damn nosey females . . .'

'I'm not,' she protested. 'After all, it is my family.'

'But it isn't, is it? You know that now. Isn't that enough?'

'No. I want to know why it irritates you so much. I want to know' . . . recklessly . . . 'what you're trying to hide.'

'Trying to hide?'

'My step-cousin Pearce Grant seemed to think so. In fact he advised me to—'

Rowan did not finish. With unnecessary force Jonathan accelerated the engine and the boat took off. He kept up the pace . . . and the noise . . . all the way back to the coast.

CHAPTER SEVEN

THE crook proved all that Jonathan had said it would, and after the foot had gone down to the doctor's satisfaction . . . another journey to the cottage hospital . . . Rowan practised hobbling around with the crutch, then, when she considered herself expert on it, she asked the trustee to do as he had said he would, drive her to the café each day.

Rather to her surprise he agreed without any of his usual argument. Sick of her? She was not aware that she asked this aloud until he answered, 'Very sick. Why not?'

She did not challenge the 'Why not?' . . . instead she said humbly, 'I'm sorry that I have to keep on offending you with my presence, but I must stick it out here. I spent my last penny coming to Australia.'

'You really mean you made a do-or-die bet of it? You took a chance?'

'Isn't life sometimes that?'

'Yes, but your coming here was entirely that.'

'Well, what did you expect? Did you think that when I heard that the scene was Australia I immediately pined for gum trees?'

'You have a sharp tongue, Miss Redland.'

'And an inquisitive nose,' she reminded him.

'Also a mean memory. Be ready in ten minutes.'

'Or you'll put your finger on the horn.'

'Or I shall go without you. I'm meeting some Southerners this morning and hoping to get their signatures to a piece of big business, so naturally little businesses can't hold me up.'

'Naturally.' She saw to it that she was dressed and outside by eight minutes.

'Good girl,' he commended. She hadn't expected that, and took the opportunity of his amiability to ask could she return to her room at the stud now. She emphasized 'stud'. To her surprise . . . and faint depletion, though she would not have admitted it . . . he agreed blandly: 'Why not?'

At the café, things were going smoothly. Barney, as always, was leaving everything in readiness before he went to the cut, Mrs. White, the timber man's wife, was very efficient, and Elissa was obviously enjoying herself, darting in and out from the kitchen, well aware of the pretty sight she made in her pink apron and pink bow. The customers, always male as they were, appreciated the feminity.

'I've had a ball,' smiled Elissa, after a rush had gone. 'And my presents, Rowan! A case of pineapples. A peeled stick of sugar cane to suck. A bag of cracked Macadamia nuts. A bouquet of orchids. And' . . . she rolled her blue eyes . . . 'a baby croc! The donor promised to take him away again when he reached a dangerous age. *That* present I did *not* accept.'

'How are the ponies going?'

'Darling, I'm a working girl, how can you expect me to know that?'

'But you go home each day.'

'Very late,' came in Mrs. White disapprovingly. 'She doesn't leave till all hours.'

'There's no need for that, Elissa.'

Elissa shrugged and did not comment.

'The ponies must be thriving,' concluded Rowan, 'otherwise Nicholas would have told you.'

'I expect so.'

'Elissa . . .' Rowan began.

'Look, Rowan, I came into this stud thing with my brother, but I'm not all that interested.'

'Yes, but you're an excellent horsewoman. Almost, I would say, a perfect one.'

Elissa did not answer for several moments, then she said bleakly... and incomprehensibly to Rowan, 'Perhaps that was the trouble.'

'What, Elissa?'

'Business, boss,' trilled Elissa, eager to escape any probing, and she went to the door to welcome the haulier burning up the motorway to pull in at Eats. Only it was not a truck. Rowan had got on to her crook and hobbled over to look, too. It was a long sleek car. In it was a good-looking, fair young man.

'We're having society,' Rowan quipped, but she said it to herself. Elissa was gone.

The man came in. He had a pleasant smile and a charming personality. He said that yes, steak and eggs would be fine.

Rowan hobbled out and told Mrs. White, and between them they fixed up the tray and brought it back.

'Having a bad spell,' said the man sympathetically. 'Can't you get anyone to help out?'

'As a matter of fact we have someone, but all at once she's gone.'

His eyes narrowed slightly, but he did not comment. He asked Rowan how she had received her injury.

'Trying to brush up the old place,' she said ruefully. 'You may not have noticed it, but we're having opposition.' She had not had time yet to notice it much herself, but a glance through the door made her feel unhappy. The new building was *very* pleasant. Prefabricated, admittedly, but attractively so. Beside The Outlook, Eats was Cinderella after the Ball.

'This is a strategic place,' reminded the customer

cheerfully, 'in time it should carry two eating houses.'

'In time.'

'It's the motorway that keeps it going, of course. There's nothing else here.'

'Only a few farms, cane, pineapple, what-have-you,' agreed Rowan, 'the mountain timber and the stud.'

'Stud?'

'Not long opened. In fact Nicholas came the day I did.'

'I see. And how is Mr. Nicholas doing?'

'That's his first name,' she smiled. 'Fine, so far. Of course it's all still rather an experiment to see whether the soft air of Queensland can come up to the apple air of New Zealand. But the grey recovered very quickly.'

'This man is a vet?'

'Yes.'

'And the grey?'

'It was attached to a rodeo troupe going through for the Corner's Golden Cup. They stopped here for dinner, mentioned to me that the grey looked seedy, and when I told them about the vet surgeon, left the grey there.'

'I see. Is he right now?'

'Before I left there, owing to my ankle incident, he was doing wonderfully. I could find out for sure, only the sister of the stud, who has been helping me, seems to have gone.' Rowan looked round her again.

'I see,' the customer said once more.

They talked easily for a while – it was the lull period of the morning – then the man got up, paid his bill, then went to the door.

'I'll probably be back,' he smiled.

'Thank you.'

'For the grey as well as for a meal.'

'For the grey? Then – you're Larry.'

He grinned. 'I see the boys have been talking. They're a

good bunch.'

'Very good.'

'I'll speak with them first, let them tell me about the grey, otherwise they might think I've been checking up on them.'

She nodded.

'But I'll be back to get the pony, to thank this Nicholas, pay him up.'

'That's good, Mr.—'

'You said the name before,' he reminded her.

'Larry,' she agreed. Then she said, 'I'm Rowan. I'll tell Nicholas, Larry. His sister, too, will be pleased. Up here there's not much contemporary company, and Elissa . . .'

'Elissa?' He was half way through the doorway now, but he turned completely round.

'That's her name. Not really common, is it?'

'Not really,' he said after a pause. When he went out he looked up and down for several long minutes almost as though he was searching for someone before he got into his car and drove off.

A pleasant person, Rowan thought.

When Barney came in that evening, and Rowan went off duty, it was to the stud she went again. No one was around, and as it was still light she walked down to the stables. How beautiful it was with the westered sun now setting behind those remarkably domed mountains to leave the eastern slopes to collect violet slabs of shadow in its blurred shapes of trees. There was a gentleness in the air that even the most cold country horses should be unable to resist, smiled Rowan as she turned into the first barn.

Because of the silky warmth, the horses were not bedded inside, though Nicholas had said the sheds might be used in bad weather. She could see several of Nicholas's 'boys' and 'girls' in different corrals. She recognized Bright Bruce, Captain, Westbound, they were having a conversation over the fence with Golden Haze and mother-to-be Miss Mary. She stood watching them a while, then began looking for Nicholas again.

She found him fussing over the foaling box.

'Because,' he said before she could ask, 'I think Miss Mary is further than I was told when I got her. Also, the old hands around here say a blow is coming.'

'Jemima,' sighed Rowan.

'They don't allot the same name twice.' He stopped his small attentions to the box, came out and took Rowan's hands. 'It's good to see you again. Quite recovered?'

'So much so that I left my walking crook at the house. I can't say I'm up to a climb in the hills, but the ankle does seem much stronger.'

'And you're back with us again?'

'If you'll have me.'

'Oh, Rowan!' was all Nicholas said.

They strolled back to the house ... the sun had slipped right over the domes now, it was almost night. Rowan told Nicholas how Larry who ran the rodeo troupe had called in at the café and learned about the grey.

'He's nice. He wouldn't come over now because he felt the boys would sooner report the incident. How is the invalid?'

'Eating his head off, absolutely fit.' They climbed the steps together. 'Elissa come with you?'

'I was going to ask you about her; she left the café all at once. I thought she'd returned here.'

'She could have, I've been outside all day. Wasn't she at home just now?'

'No. Perhaps she is by now.' Rowan called, 'Elissa, you have your old boarder back again!'

There was no reply.

Rowan made coffee, and since Mrs. White had left

Nicholas a midday meal and he was not all that hungry, she toasted sandwiches, and they sat on the verandah and ate them.

'Where is that girl?' Nicholas grumbled, though not over-concerned.

'There's nowhere for her here,' Rowan said more dubiously. She was concerned.

At nine o'clock she suggested to Nicholas that he check the car to see if it was there, then went with him while he did so. The car stood beside the new truck. Nicholas turned to hunch his shoulders at Rowan.

'Have you looked in her room?'

'You do that, Rowan. Women can tell better than men what gives.'

But anyone could have told, for Elissa had left a note. Typical of that impetuous girl, she had written: 'Buzzed down to Brisbane to buy a few things. Back some time. E.'

'Down to Brisbane,' said Nicholas. 'It's a wonder she didn't make it Sydney, Melbourne. Knowing my young sister it's a wonder she didn't fly to Paris.'

'. . . How well do you know her?' Rowan asked deliberately.

Nicholas looked at Rowan. 'What do you mean?'

'I don't know myself . . . I mean it was nothing really.' But something was nagging at Rowan. One moment Elissa had stood beside her at the café, and the next minute she was gone. Why? Had she seen someone and didn't want them to see her? Who had it been? She tried to remember. The truckie, perhaps, who had brought her a baby croc and promptly been handed it back again? No, Elissa would make fun out of that. Maybe one of the knights of the road who had not been very knightly, but Elissa, Rowan felt sure, could look after herself.

'How would she get away?' Nicholas was saying, angry

now. 'There's only one way, that wretched girl has hitched a hike.'

'She'll be all right,' soothed Rowan, but she felt cross, too, with Elissa. It was the only way, as Nicholas had just said, that she could go, but it wasn't the right way, it was the unadvised way. She agreed with Nicholas when he said next:

'That girl needs a firm hand.'

Rowan made coffee again, then said she supposed she better get going.

'Going where?'

'To Narganoo. To the trustee.'

'But you've returned here. I heard you call out that the old boarder was back again.'

'There was no Elissa to hear, for which reason, Nicholas, I have to go now.'

At his incredulous look she repeated what Jonathan had said about sophisticated states.

'You didn't take him seriously?'

'I take my present rather precarious position very seriously, Nicholas. You see, I don't want to make any mistakes for the simple reason that I don't want to leave this part of the world.'

'There are other ways of remaining,' Nicholas said quietly. – Jonathan had said that. He had added in his bitter way: 'Like marrying the vet.' Then he had inquired if Nicholas had asked her and she had tossed back, more to annoy than answer him: 'Not in so many words.'

But the words Nicholas used now were direct.

'Elissa will always be a feather in the wind, she'll come and she'll go. Anyway, probably she'll marry and leave. I hope so. – Rowan—' A pause. 'Rowan—'

'No, Nicholas,' she said before he asked.

'I've put it unromantically, haven't I? I put the reasons, but not what a girl wants to hear.'

'That's the whole trouble, Nicholas, I don't want to hear.'

'You mean—' he said unhappily.

'Yes, I mean that, Nicholas.'

He thought it out a while, then said cheerfully, for he was essentially a cheerful soul: 'Then that settles you returning to Saxby's tonight, doesn't it? With an understanding between us like that there's no reason on earth for me to get out the car.'

'Oh, Nicholas!' She had to laugh at him. 'A "reason" doesn't come into it. I mean I'll still be subject to Jonathan Saxby's approval whether there's an understanding between us two or not, so I must go back.'

'Only a fool would listen to you,' Nicholas sighed, getting up nevertheless to pick up the car keys.

They drove down the motorway to the turn-off to Narganoo. The cane fires were burning, and Rowan remembered her first night and her alarm at the flames. Nicholas was intrigued with the ginger crop. He put the headlights on one of the fields and got out to examine it.

But when he got to the homestead, he would not wait. 'In these relaxed days I'd feel a fool handing over a woman just because my own domicile was short of a female chaperone.'

'I know,' Rowan giggled, 'but it's all for a good cause.'

But when she went inside it was to find that Jonathan was not there; the deal with the Southerners must be a lengthy one. She talked with Nancy until Nancy made supper, and then went to bed.

Some time in the night she vaguely heard a car returning, but it did not register. The first thing that did register was a 'Rise and shine', and Jonathan standing there with the breakfast tray, just as he had that first morning.

As he checked the tea, toast, butter, golden ginger marmalade . . . and a shoot of red ginger blossom . . . he said boyishly, 'I got the contracts.'

'Congratulations.'

He looked down on the tray again. 'I did it myself,' he nodded. 'Though you wouldn't know the difference in these bright skies, it's actually quite early. Barely sun-up. Nancy isn't out yet.'

'It looks all right to me,' said Rowan of her breakfast. A pause. 'Do I eat the ginger?'

'The ginger spread?'

'The shoot of ginger.'

'That,' he awarded, 'is for being a good girl.'

'For not stopping at the stud because Elissa's gone.'

'Has she?'

Irritably Rowan said, 'Why otherwise would I have come back here?'

'To see me?' he suggested idly.

'I came because of what you said.' As he still stood there, she added: 'Propriety.'

'And Nicholas swallowed that!'

'I'm here, aren't I?'

'Yes . . . but you wouldn't be if *I* was Jarvis.'

Not waiting for the indignant response he knew must come, he went blandly out.

Annoyed with him yet unable not to laugh. Rowan took up the red plant and sniffed its pungency. The ginger shoot *was* that man, she thought.

She managed that day without the crook, and the ankle behaved well. They were not over-busy, so she had time to observe The Outlook, which was being fitted up now, though still was not to the stage of accepting customers.

During the afternoon several cars pulled up, and three

women and two men got out. They would be her step-cousins, she guessed. It seemed to Rowan very petty not to recognize them. Although her family eagerness had diminished once she had learned that these cousins were no blood relation ... and once she had encountered Pearce ... it still seemed chary not to say hullo. She went across.

They were civil, but there was no warmth there.

'Your grandmother,' one of the women related coolly, 'brought your mother with her to the second marriage. The child was very young, much younger than our parents, and later, when your grandmother died, our grandfather put your mother into boarding school. We seldom saw her, so of course ...' She shrugged.

So of course, interpreted Rowan, there was no bond was what she meant.

'Then she grew up, married and went to England.' Another shrug. 'Why our Uncle Thomas should have chosen you is incomprehensible. There's no blood connection at all.'

'Why didn't you object legally?' Rowan had asked this of Pearce, and now she received a similar reply.

'Law!' scoffed her step-cousin.

Another step-cousin joined his sister. 'Why didn't you listen to reason?' Hal ... she deduced it was Hal ... asked Rowan. 'It would have saved all this trouble.'

'I wanted the place,' Rowan admitted.

'You won't get it, you know. On the terms of the will you have to keep up the profits, and once we're in swing you'll find the takings are going down.'

'Is it that big an inheritance to fight so hard?' Rowan asked.

'We could ask that of you.'

'But I'm one and you are five.'

'Six,' said one of the step-cousins.

Pearce had strolled across, and he was looking appreciatively at Rowan. 'Rowan doesn't know much about the family,' he said. 'Let her discover for herself.'

'But—'

'Let her find out. Now, Rowan, if you're still sure you're not interested in that little consideration I mentioned—'

'I am not interested,' Rowan said, and turned back again. She could see now why Uncle Thomas had passed over his nieces and nephews, five ... six ... of them. *Six?* They were not types you could react to, no comfort there, no giving, only taking. No warm pungent ginger. Now why had she said that?

She returned to the café and got on to the sandwiches. Mrs. White was back at the stud again, preparing Nicholas's meal, doing the house, going home of a night. Rowan wondered how long Elissa would stop away.

She was an odd girl, she thought, buttering busily. For all her flippant outlook, Rowan believed there was something else there. But her present disappearing prank did not back that up.

During the afternoon, the troupe boys came down with a float to pick up the grey. Larry was with them in his sports car. They all had a meal at Tom Thumb, which helped her profits considerably, then drove along to the stud. When later they returned, Larry sent the float on, then got out of the car and came across to the café.

'All well?' Rowan asked.

'Splendid. Grey was in good hands.'

'You'll remember that when you have another job?'

'What is this?' he smiled. 'You seem very interested.'

'Nicholas deserves patronage starting out like this.'

'I agree with you. Not even a woman's touch to help out.'

'There is,' said Rowan, 'but she's away now.'

'Oh, yes, you mentioned a sister.' He paused. 'Elissa.'

'You have a good memory.'

'For some things.' She thought he seemed to put an emphasis on that. He asked offhandedly, 'When will she get back?'

Rowan said she did not know, glancing curiously at him as she answered. He must have noticed her curiosity, for he dismissed, 'It's just that I had some tickets.'

'Another rodeo coming up?'

'Yes. Not a "corner" this time. Brudwick. Further west. It'll be a good show. There's to be a novice . . . a first side ever.'

'I don't like the sound of that. It could be dangerous.'

'Everything is dangerous one way or other. Here are the tickets, Rowan. Try to come.'

'And bring Elissa?' She did not know what prompted her to say that.

He looked at her a long moment. Once he wet his lips as though to say something. But when he did speak all he said was: 'Yes. Why not?'

When Barney came in he told Rowan that tomorrow was her stand-down day.

'I have no place to stand down, I think I'll work.'

'No,' said Barney.

'The trustee wouldn't like it?'

'I wouldn't either. I mean . . . Well, your off day is Nancy's day.'

Rowan said carefully, 'And Nancy matters, doesn't she, Barney?' When the man did not answer, she went on, 'I think you had a dream about this café, and it included Nancy.'

'Now, Rowan—'

'I've spoiled it, haven't I?'

'Of course not, if it hadn't been you it had to be them, which heaven forbid, but whatever it was, it couldn't be us.'

123

'Did it have to matter? I mean, Barney, if you love Nancy—'

But Barney had gone a vivid red, and Rowan knew she had made a mistake. That pair were not in their greening, and what lay between them was still unexpressed . . . would remain unexpressed. And yet, Rowan knew, it would be *there*. She believed she understood the position. Barney had dreamed of this place for *his* place – and *Nancy's* place. Now that the dream was gone he couldn't fit in the scattered pieces. Perhaps he would in time, but he wasn't young, and it had been a dream too long. Oh, Uncle Thomas, why did you die when you did, she thought, before you could make a sensible will? Or better still sell to Barney.

She supposed she had better set off for Narganoo since the stud was still womanless. She would take a lift to the gate, then walk along the long track.

There was no trouble in hitch-hiking to the archway leading to the ginger farm, though a little trouble in convincing the driver that she would be bad company stopping on with him right to his destination, another seven hundred miles. Laughing at him, she got out.

It was a beautiful calm night, but rather dark for up here. The usual bright stars . . . for in these latitudes the stars were very bright . . . were cloud-enshrouded, and the trees that bordered the long drive, bauhinias and flame, were closely planted, so that their interlocking branches shut out all but snippets of the sky. For a while the flame of a distant cane fire reflected its light and helped her a little, but the fire went out and it became quite dark. She found it hard to keep to the track. She began to think of snakes warming their bellies after the sun had gone down on sandy paths, and treading on a root, or a fallen branch, or something, she leapt forward and ran blindly for quite a few minutes . . . then found herself off the drive.

She was in the ginger, she supposed, but where in those stretching acres of ginger she did not know. It was useless looking for the lights of the homestead, for the house was set a mile, perhaps more, from the motorway. She sat down on the earth and wondered what she could do. One thing, she would not perish in silky air like this, but it was still early, and the idea of remaining here all night was a scary one.

All night it could be, too, for when she did not turn up Jonathan and Nancy would just assume that she had gone to the stud.

If only the stars would come out she would try to find her way back to the track. Once she was there she would be all right. It was ridiculous being lost on a farm, and for a moment she thought how the Grimbell girls would laugh incredulously, but then the Grimbell girls did not know how big were these places in this tall state.

She must have been there an hour when she saw a light. It was the light of a car travelling along the drive. She thought ruefully that had she not seen it she would have said that the track was in another direction. But it was on the left, and two fields away. Goodness, had she stumbled that far? She wondered how many ginger plants she had disturbed and what the ginger man would say.

But all that mattered now was getting back. Watching the light for as long as she could, and which was not long, for the track was winding and the light soon cut out, she noted the location and stumbled back again. She was so thankful when she felt sand, not cultivation, underfoot, that she did not wait to take a rest, she followed the memory of that lost light.

She walked on and on. She had known the drive was long, but never this long. When would she see Narganoo's light? Of course the going was slow, for she literally had to feel the path. She kept wondering if the next feel would have a slithery feel as well, if a snake would weave away, or worse still if it—

She hurried on, but more cautiously this time, no more blind plunging into the crop. It was much too far, though . . . or was it her slow feeling pace making it seem such a distance? Oh, why didn't the lights of home show up? Home. Why had she thought that?

Then lights *were* showing. Two beams caught her and held her there. A car turned a corner and pulled up directly in front of her.

She was sobbing hysterically as she ran forward, but Jonathan, for it was the trustee, when he reached her, just took and shook her. And shook her.

Then he kissed her.

CHAPTER EIGHT

SHE was still crying, so she supposed vaguely that that was why he had stopped his shaking and comforted her instead, for no man can abide a weeping woman. Yet if that was his idea of comfort, it was not hers, not that hard telling kiss. It was more . . . more . . .

In the darkness, Rowan's cheeks suddenly burned.

He had released her, but seeing her unsteadiness he still kept a hand on her shoulder. 'You've had me at my wits' end,' he accused. 'Why did you do such a damnfool thing?'

'You told me I had to sleep here.'

'Yes, but I didn't tell you to hitch a ride to do so. Good heavens, girl, you had only to cross to the phone and ring me and I would have come. But any phone calls are for the vet, aren't they? What happened tonight – wasn't he there?'

'I didn't ring Nicholas and it never occurred to me to ring him. When the haulier asked me could he give me a lift, I just said yes. I mean, when Narganoo was so close—'

' "So close," as you put it, in a locked cabin could turn out hundreds of miles away if the fellow hadn't stopped and you couldn't get out, so how close would you have been then?'

'It didn't happen,' she said stubbornly. Triumphantly she added, 'The man had eaten at Tom Thumb.'

'Which instantly makes him above reproach? Grow up, girl! We've a fair to good record up here, but not all motorways have good records, and our turn could come. Young females who hitch a ride are asking for trouble.'

'No trouble happened.'

'No thanks to you.' He looked at her keenly. 'Thanks to the driver?' he probed.

'He was all right.'

'He didn't even suggest that you stop on?'

The eyes were boring into Rowan's, and Rowan blurted, 'Well—'

'You see.' He was taking out his bush cigarettes.

'He was joking!' She almost screamed at him. 'I said that this was where I wanted to get off, and he let me off.'

'Yes, I know that . . . *now*.'

'Of course you know it. Aren't I here?'

'I knew before I saw you, because I questioned that truckie.'

'You what?' She was appalled.

'Barney thought you were off to the stud, so he took no notice when you left. But he happened to glimpse you in the truck cabin as the truck moved off, so he got the number. Then he rang me.'

'And you?'

'I rang the police.'

'Oh, no!' said Rowan, distressed.

'Now you see what trouble you caused by being a damn idiot.'

'That poor driver,' regretted Rowan, for though she had no doubt the man would have been pleased had she agreed to travel farther, he had still shrugged and laughed when she had declined.

'Spare your pity,' advised Jonathan. 'He was unconcerned, hauliers are tough stuff. They have to be.'

'But he would be embarrassed.'

'Not him. If anyone was, I was, having to ask the police to check. What fool sort of girl must they have thought I was inquiring about?'

'Elissa took a lift,' Rowan tried to defend herself.

'Elissa is not my concern.'

'Well, she's Nicholas's, and he didn't make such a fuss.'

'I don't think,' said Jonathan unexpectedly, 'she's her brother's concern, either.'

'What do you mean?'

'Put it down to male deduction. A man always knows whether a woman is . . . well . . .'

'Yes?'

'There,' he said cryptically, or cryptic it was to Rowan.

'What on earth do you mean?'

'I mean that Elissa is – bespoken. That's a funny fuddy old word, isn't it, bespoken. I think she's somebody else's concern.'

'But she came up here to get someone, a cane farmer, a pineapple grower.' Rowan added deliberately: 'A ginger man.'

'Jarvis's words, and not, I would say, ever backed up by Elissa herself.'

Rowan, thinking back, reluctantly had to agree with Jonathan. Elissa liked to be with men, but never, it had seemed, a man; she was coquettish with them all, but never with one. Was this then that something about Nicholas's sister she could never quite put a finger on? Could Elissa be . . . what was that old-fashioned word? . . . bespoken? Rowan was unaware of her deep concentration until Jonathan said with contempt, 'So much for male versus female intuition. Nicholas was not making a fuss because he knew . . . unconsciously perhaps . . . that it was out of his hands.'

'And you're making a fuss because I'm not? Because you're the trustee?'

'Could be.' He had finished the moulding of the cigarette, finished the licking of the edges of the paper together, and now he was lighting up. She heard the scratch of the match, then for a moment his face was clear before her, a little craggy, a little hard. Very male.

'I meant every shake I gave to you, Rowan,' he said coolly, blowing out the match and leaving them in darkness again.

'And what came after?' – Why had she asked that?

'You draw your own conclusions,' he suggested. 'Put it down to relief at not having to attend a coroner's court, or to not having to spend the rest of the night looking for you, or—'

She waited. She waited quite a long time.

'Just reach your own conclusions,' he flung at last, and his voice had a rough edge.

A little disconcerted, Rowan said, 'I think I may have damaged some of your ginger.'

'How in tarnation did you get into the ginger?'

'I thought I trod on a snake . . . I suppose it was a root . . . but I jumped and kept running, and then I was off the drive. It was dark and I couldn't see and I just kept on. I was two fields away when I saw a car going along the avenue to Narganoo.'

'That was me coming *from* Narganoo to see if you'd turned up yet. When you hadn't I came back again, or at least I got this far.'

'Then I wasn't walking home. I mean' . . . hoping he had not heard that "home" . . . 'I was walking away from the homestead.'

'You were walking away from the home*stead*.' There was the slightest emphasis there, he must have noticed her first slip. 'You would have walked right on to the motorway, either under or into a truck. So much for your bump of locality!'

I'm not a local.'

'No,' he agreed.

The clouds that had been obliterating the stars all the night were speeding away. In the sudden clarity Rowan saw that Jonathan was looking intently at her. 'Just don't do that again,' he said.

'Or?'

'Or I'd say you were a glutton for punishment, because I'd do the same as I just did.' He paused intentionally. '*All* of it. You can take that as a promise . . . or a threat. Just please yourself. Now get into the car and I'll take you' . . . he waited a moment . . . 'to the homestead.'

Long after she had gone to bed, even though Nancy brought a glass of hot milk, Rowan stared through the window at the ginger fields, now illumined brightly by stars that had previously refused to help her out. Sleep would not come.

Little things came back to her to send her cheeks flushing vividly. That hard, telling kiss. That face in the light of a match, craggy . . . male. Jonathan Saxby's 'I'd do the same as I just did. All of it. You can take that as a promise . . . or a threat.'

What had he meant? Or was nothing meant? When all this was ended, as it must end, what would the end be?

'Rise and shine!' He was standing with the tray, so at some time she must have fallen asleep.

Rowan glanced to the window and though up here the sun, once it broke through, simply shone, no hourly progressions, she could tell she was late. She said so.

'No,' he reminded her, 'it's your day off, and I'm taking you out. That bump of locality, lack of, last night gave me food for thought. I don't believe you have a clue where you are up here.'

She was looking down at the tray, seeing no ginger

blossom.

'Is a bump of locality necessary?' she asked.

'It helps.'

'When one is temporary?'

'Given up the struggle already?'

She did not comment on that, and presently he said, 'I think you should know more about this tall state, if only to tell your friends when you get back to England. I give you—'

'Thirty minutes.' She beat him to it. As he went out, she called, 'Thanks for the tray. – But no ginger blossom?'

'I reckoned you'd had more than enough of that last night.'

She ate and drank quickly, dressed quickly. She knew by now that so many minutes to Jonathan Saxby was so many minutes, not one second more.

She was out by the first pressure of his finger on the horn.

'Where are we going?' she asked.

'A surprise.'

She looked at the less than young morning. 'I can't see that I'll get much of a locality bump, not at this time of day. You should have wakened me earlier.'

'The idea did occur to me, but I thought you would be tuckered out after last night's episode and need the sleep. However, what I have in mind won't take long, and will give you a very good idea.' He touched the switch and began moving the car down the drive.

When they emerged to the motorway they turned neither left towards the café nor right which led to the northern towns. Jonathan went straight ahead down a bumpy road. 'This is the back way in,' he said.

'To where?'

'Our airfield.' Proudly.

'Airfield? ... Then—'

'We're going up. I'm friends with the flying instructor here. You're really going to see the place.'

When they reached the airfield, Rowan found it was quite small.

'Yes,' nodded Jonathan, 'it's a club. I belong myself. Actually I could take you up myself, but on this occasion I want to show you, so I've asked Guy to do the honours.'

Guy, pleasant, relaxed, sauntered across to the car, then led them to the little Dragon that waited on a narrow strip in the middle of a paddock of bleached grass and thriving thistle. Rowan was legged up.

It was a wonderful experience. Guy followed the motorway north when Jonathan told him that Rowan would already have seen the aspect from the south.

She looked down on chocolate . . . for that was the soil required for cane . . . earth and damply shining sugar shoots, but Guy called slyly that the main colours up here were black and red, black from the black molasses, red from Nelson's blood, the red rum. 'Cane produces both,' he grinned, 'as well as lollipops.'

She saw trains going through the main streets of towns, forests of bunya, cypress, kauri and Indian teak. She saw to the east the never-ending islands of the Reef.

'And so it goes on,' said Jonathan when they came down again, 'right up to finger point, which, as you might guess, is up top.'

They had a cup of tea with the pilot, Rowan thanking him again for the wonderful experience. She thanked Jonathan as they went back to the car.

'It's not finished yet,' he said.

He took a different track out of the airfield, and presently Rowan saw they were climbing. She was elated; she had wanted to go into the mountains.

'The domes and the pinnacles that Captain Cook saw

have petered out at this stage,' Jonathan related, 'but it's still a relation of the same range. I think this point will give us a view while we eat.'

Nancy had packed a delightful lunch and flasks of tea.

'Sacrilege,' sighed Jonathan of the flasks, 'with all these gum twigs around, but instant tea is a time-saver.'

They talked very little during the meal. Rowan for her part was content simply to sit and look out, and Jonathan seemed to be occupied with his thoughts. It was only when he had rolled and lit his cigarette that he began to speak.

'I wanted you to get an idea of the place for another reason other than getting a bump of locality.'

'Yes?'

'I wanted to bring you here so you could understand.'

'Understand what?'

He had taken out a pencil and a notebook, and he was making a quick sketch. 'Understand this,' he said.

He had drawn a long straight line that she gathered even before he indicated it was their motorway. He put two crosses on it, almost opposite each other.

'Tom Thumb,' he tapped with his pencil. 'The Outlook.' Another tap. 'In other words, you and the opposition.'

'Yes?'

'Being an intelligent girl ... now you needn't look coy, I think you're aware that you're no fool ... you must have been wondering why.'

'Why?'

'Why two sections of people are wrangling over one spot.'

'I'm sure I'm not wrangling.'

He ignored that.

'I think you must have wondered why a wretched little place like Eats has five people breathing fire to get **at** it.'

'Six,' she said. 'That's what I heard.'

He gave her a sharp look, but again ignored her.

'There's no doubt that a windfall, a money windfall, is pleasant, however small. Still, I don't think that the Tom Thumb as it is would have raised the interest that it has but for what's going to happen.'

'Yes?'

'Watch the sketch,' he directed, and he drew a line from the west to join the motorway. It met at almost their own cross, the Tom Thumb cross.

'Another motorway,' he said.

'And it connects right there?'

'Precisely. But' ... scoring out The Outlook ... 'not there. In fact, with the clover-leaves the road builders put in these days that X marking that spot will be wiped right out.'

'I see.'

He put down the sketch. '*Do* you see?' he said sharply. 'Do you see the goldmine you're sitting on?'

'Or falling off, more like it.'

'Perhaps, but at least you understand the position. These people, these step-cousins of yours, are not just money-grabbing, they're *big* money-grabbing, and for a position like that' ... he glanced down at the Tom Thumb cross ... 'I don't blame them.'

'No,' said Rowan fairly, 'I don't either, and I'm glad you told me.'

She sat silent a while, then she said, 'Poor Barney, he would have been a rich man if Uncle Tom had sold out to him.'

'Barney wouldn't have wanted that. All he ever wanted was a place by the roadside and Nancy to help him run it.'

'Then at least he can have Nancy.'

'No.'

'No?'

Jonathan was silent a while. 'I don't think you'd understand if I told you.'

'I'd try.'

'Well, Barney is of the old school. I have no doubt in all these years he has got no further with Nancy than a long look once a week over a tray of steak.'

'Oh, surely—'

'I told you that you wouldn't understand. To men like Barney something to show is their song of love. The caff was to be Barney's song of love.'

'And now,' said Rowan sadly, 'the notes are gone.'

'You're not laughing?'

'Oh, no, I like Barney. I like Nancy. It's easy for me, a different generation, a wider background, or' . . . looking down and out . . . 'a more sophisticated one, to say "How ridiculous", but I haven't lived all my life in the same spot.'

'Almost the same field, you could say. Barney was no itinerant canecutter hitting south with a wad at the end of a season. He simply stayed on.' A pause. 'And on.'

'And Nancy was always here?'

'Always with me. With my – mother before me.' Again that slight pause she had noticed before from Jonathan. 'Oh, Barney could storm Nancy all right, but it simply wouldn't occur to him. It wouldn't occur to her to encourage it. I've no doubt the romantic proposal he always intended was: "I'll be needing someone permanent in the caff, Nance, how about it?" ' Jonathan laughed ruefully. 'I only wish I could put some dynamite under that stubborn cuss!'

'I wish I could help,' Rowan said.

They packed up soon afterwards and descended from

the mountains again.

The next morning Jonathan drove her to work as usual, then wasted no time in getting to his own business, since although the ginger harvesting and preparing were finished, the packaging and bottling was now in full swing, and demanding all his attention.

Barney, ready to go to the cut, greeted Rowan with his usual report on the number of cut sandwiches he had prepared, told her it had been a fair to middling night, then set off.

Rowan wandered round her rather odd little domain. Yet not so odd now as when she first had arrived, and definitely, although it could not compare to the opposition, such a horror.

Customers were a little tardy, and she wondered if her step-cousins had opened shop. She peered out, but saw the carpenters still at work ... she also saw a truck coming down the motorway and veering inwards as they did when they were preparing to stop. She went in and threw on a steak.

But hardly had the brakes screamed to a halt than the truck started off once more. There was brief laughter, a high musical, 'Thanks a lot, safe journey,' then Elissa breezed in. She looked very lovely in a scarlet pants suit with cheeks and lips to match.

'No need for any cooking,' she tossed. 'Bruce and I ate further down.'

'Bruce who?'

'How should I know, and for heaven's sake, Rowan, get that schoolmarm note out of your voice!'

Rowan bit her lip and did not answer back. But she could not let the episode pass without some comment. She said gently, 'Elissa, is it wise?'

'Is what wise?'

'Hitch-hiking and I'm not speaking as a schoolmarm, I'm speaking as one who did it myself several nights ago.' She paused. 'And got into trouble.'

'Well, the difference between us, Rowan, is I won't get into trouble.'

'Nicholas—'

'Couldn't care less. No, that's not right, actually, he just accepts me as not his responsibility.'

'Because you're of age?'

'No, I don't think so. It's just that, although he doesn't know anything – well, anything concrete – I still believe something in him is resigned to it.'

'Elissa, what are you talking about?'

'Sheer nonsense. Haven't you gathered yet that I'm a nonsensical person? And don't you want to see what I bought in the big city?' She opened her bag to tumble out frivolous things. 'Presents, too. A cravat for Nick seeing he's given up ties, and some fetching aprons for you.' She tossed out several rainbow-coloured items. 'You must have noticed,' she giggled, 'what they did for me.'

'Yes,' said Rowan abstractedly, 'a pineapple, a stick of cane, a baby croc and a lot of wistful looks.'

'Well, that's nice,' defended Elissa.

'Only not important,' dared Rowan.

'Those things never are,' agreed Elissa carelessly.

'Especially when you're not interested, especially when your interest has been' . . . what was Jonathan's 'old-fashioned' word? . . . 'bespoken.'

Elissa turned sharply on her. 'Now what are *you* talking about?' she said in her turn.

'Simply a remark, Elissa. I've always had the impression that though you're having fun, you're not terribly amused, that it actually means nothing to you.'

'You think too much, Rowan,' dismissed Elissa. 'Please can I have a cup of tea?'

Over the tea, Rowan said, 'You went in a hurry. One minute you were here, the next you were gone.'

'That's Elissa,' Elissa said blandly.

'I think it is. What got into you?'

'Sudden impulse ... plus an invitation from a big hunk of a haulier who was going right through to Brisbane. You have to decide quickly.'

'One day you'll decide too quickly,' warned Rowan, but she was stopped by Elissa's mischievous face near hers demanding what Rowan's hitch had been like and what trouble she had got into. 'Trouble from whom?'

'Jonathan Saxby.'

'I'm consumed with envy! He's pure ginger, that ginger man. I was hoping that it was Nicholas who blew you up.'

'Why?'

'For all your faults,' Elissa grinned impishly, 'I could stand you for a sister.'

'No,' refused Rowan, but kindly.

'I rather expected so. Also, I rather believe Nick is married to his stud.' She got up and wandered round the café ... then, abruptly, she stopped.

'More rodeo tickets?' Her voice was sharp.

'Yes. They were left here when the troupe came down to collect the grey.'

'So the grey has gone?'

'Yes,' said Rowan again. 'The boss of the outfit came, too. He was very pleased with everything.'

'The boss. The one called—'

'Called Larry,' Rowan said.

'Then they all left again?'

'After giving me these tickets.'

'Well, I don't know about you, Rowan, but I've had enough rodeos.'

Rowan nodded agreement. 'Though this one,' she admitted, 'is different.'

'How can it be different? They do the same things.'

'This one includes a novice competition. It's reserved for competitors who've never rough-ridden before.'

There was a dead silence. Glancing up, Rowan was shocked at the pallor on Elissa's face. The cheeks that had matched the scarlet pants suit were drained of colour, the cherry lips only showed red where Elissa was biting them.

'Are you all right?' she asked.

'Of course I'm all right. A bit dizzy, that big hunk of a haulier certainly burned up the miles.' As she was replying, Elissa was reaching for the tickets again, re-reading them.

'Novice,' she said expressionlessly.

'Yes.'

'Next Wednesday.'

'Yes.'

'Of course I won't go.'

'No,' agreed Rowan, wondering why a ticket for a rodeo all at once seemed to electrify the room.

'Elissa—' She half-stepped forward.

'I'd better go and report my safe return to my dear brother,' evaded Elissa. 'See you tonight, Rowan.' She ran up the track to the stud.

Fortunately, both for business as well as Rowan's branching thoughts, the dinner hour trucks began pulling in, and for the next few hours she had no time for anything but steaks. Then today the earlier teas came almost on top of the late dinners, which meant that she was busy right until Barney came.

'A good day,' he said with satisfaction as he looked in the till. Although it was not his caff, he was always pleased when business was brisk.

Rowan stopped for a while to finish some sandwiches

she hadn't had time to complete, said a little diffidently that she was sorry about the hitch-hike incident and she wouldn't do it again, then set off to the stud. At the door she informed Barney very circumspectly that Miss Jarvis was back again, thinking as she did so that she hadn't informed the maker of that law, the big boss at Narganoo. Well, the ginger man could find it out for himself.

When she reached the stud she saw that Elissa had changed into her jodhpurs and was exercising Captain. She crossed to where Nicholas leaned over a rail watching his sister, and commented, 'She's certainly a remarkable horsewoman.'

'She's certainly driving me to distraction, or rather she's driving Captain,' Nicholas corrected grimly. 'I told her to canter the stallion, not blaze a trail like that. The boy's not used to it yet. He's had the long journey up from Melbourne, and now he needs to loosen gradually, not explode – Elissa! *Elissa!* For heaven's sake!'

Elissa came galloping over, all sweetness and light. 'Yes, dear brother?'

'If you can't obey me, then leave the horse alone.'

'Obedience.' Elissa pretended to consider the word a moment. 'Obedience. Man's prerogative ... from a woman. No, I won't obey you, Nick. On the other hand I'm sick of riding.' She slid off, handing Rowan the reins. The two of them, Nicholas and Rowan, watched her saunter off.

'She can be the devil,' Nicholas fumed.

'Why, Nicholas?' Rowan felt she knew Nicholas enough now to ask that outright.

'To tell you the truth I don't know. She wasn't always like this. Impulsive, yes, a bit of a scatterbrain, but not ... well ...'

'Driven?' suggested Rowan. 'Driven in this instance to drive Captain simply because she had to release something?'

'Exactly,' nodded Nicholas. 'But I don't know why.'

Backing up Elissa's words that Elissa's brother, though unconsciously, no longer accepted her as his responsibility, Nicholas now took hold of Rowan's arm and led her to the barn. All the way there he talked eagerly about Miss Mary, Elissa obviously forgotten.

'I'm sure now she's much further,' he said. 'I don't want to be a bore to you, Rowan—'

'You're not a bore.'

'But this first foaling both for the stud and for Miss Mary will mean a lot to me. I'll feel I have established something. Do you think she looks well?'

'She looks wonderful.'

'Not a little droopy?'

'Wonderful.'

'Not a little—'

Their eyes met and they both laughed. 'Talk about a mother hen!' Rowan accused.

'Father rooster,' he corrected, 'the mother hen hasn't eventuated. Rowan . . .'

Rowan anticipated the trend. 'Nicholas, of all the un-romantic passes!'

'But you know what I mean.'

'Yes.' She turned and patted his cheek. 'Only I think it's like your sister said, first of all it's the stud.'

He did not attempt to deny that. He patted her cheek back, and companionably they walked to the homestead.

Elissa had quietened down, she even had laid the table for the meal that Mrs. White had left prepared. She gave Nicholas his present, and he thanked and kissed her, but could not resist adding that a kiss was more than she deserved.

'Captain enjoyed that gallop,' she tossed back at him.

She paused. 'So did I.'

Nicholas looked at Rowan wryly, a glance that wondered if his sister at this present incomprehensible stage was enjoying anything.

They had their meal on the verandah, then after the night fell still sat on. They were sitting there when the car came up the track.

The first thing that Rowan thought was: Jonathan believes I'm missing again, and has come to find out. But she need not have feared, nor even have considered herself as featuring in Jonathan's thoughts, for it was the sleek model of the rodeo troupe boss, not the Narganoo car.

Nicholas had got up and gone down the steps to greet the visitor.

'It will be Larry,' Rowan said to Elissa, then saw, as before ... and hadn't that been on such an occasion? ... that Elissa was not there. It's odd, she thought.

But no one commented on Elissa's absence. She herself avoided it, Nicholas obviously did not think about it, Larry—

Larry? He certainly did not look around, he certainly asked no questions, but Rowan was definitely aware of a seeking in him somewhere, a kind of reaching out. Again she thought: It's odd.

Nicholas was very happy. Larry wanted him to stable a bunch of his ponies at the stud for a resting spell. It would be a boost to the infant stud business, Rowan saw, and she was glad for Nicholas.

She got up and made coffee ... still no mention of Elissa. The girl had not entered the conversation once when Larry rose at length and left.

Nicholas, too, did not ask about her. He sat on talking for a while, obviously bucked by the unexpected windfall.

'I'll have to make a new corral,' he planned, 'keep the

bunch separate. Do you mind, Rowan, I'll get to bed now, no more chatter. Busy day tomorrow.'

She smiled at him and his plans, but she did not move off to bed herself.

Where was Elissa? She checked on the girl's room again. It was empty, the bed untouched. Quietly she went to the garage, and saw that the car had gone. She had not heard it, but that could easily happen as the garages were away from the house.

For a few moment she stood uncertain. She did not want to cut into Nicholas's pleasant preoccupation with his stud. On the other hand Elissa was not here.

Then she remembered Jonathan. Twice now he had pulled her up for not going to him with her troubles. 'You have only to cross to the phone,' he had said.

But she couldn't cross here, Nicholas would hear. Silently she ran down the track. As she went she planned what she would say. Instead of bursting out: 'Elissa is gone,' she first would inform him that she was staying at the stud again now that there was a female third. Then from that juncture she would . . .

Typical of Barney, he made no comment on a girl running down a track to ring up when she could have rung at the house. He gave her the Narganoo number, then bustled in to take an order from a late lone truck.

Jonathan's voice came back over the wire. 'Narganoo here.'

'It's Rowan. Rowan Redland.'

'Yes?'

'I – I wanted to tell you I wouldn't be there tonight.'

'Bit tardy, aren't you?'

'Better late than never.' She tried to make light going of it.

'I agree. But as it has happened you needn't have bothered. I knew.'

'Knew?' she echoed.

'Elissa told me you were there.'

'Elissa . . . where is Elissa?'

'Here.'

'At Narganoo?'

'Yes.' A pause. 'As a matter of fact, in your room.'

Frigidly Rowan said, 'I have no room.'

'Well' . . . impatiently . . . 'the guest room you've occupied.'

'Is she – staying?'

'I've had a long day, I don't intend conducting her back.'

'I've had a long day, too, I don't intend to come over to accompany her. Nor does her brother.'

'Very well, then. Was there anything else?'

Anything else! This pompous impossible man who had made an outmoded rule that nowhere else in the wide world . . . yes, *truly* . . . would such a rule not be greeted with incredulous guffaws, now just as complacently, and very conveniently, cancelling the rule.

'I'll be remaining at the stud,' she said levelly.

'Yes.'

'But you said . . .' Yet she could not say it, she had never been so angry in her life.

'Anything else, Miss Redland?' He waited a moment, then finished casually, 'Good night.'

The phone went down.

Without a word to Barney, Rowan went back along the track.

CHAPTER NINE

SHE lay looking at Nicholas's barns changed by the moonlight into silvery shapes, beyond the barns at the star-shadowed paddocks, then beyond the paddocks at an obscure violet slab that would be the now night-hidden range.

But she was not looking out on ginger fields.

She thought of Elissa at Narganoo, lovely Elissa of whom the trustee had said that first day when she had asked him pointedly if Nicholas was up to his requirements, a succinct: 'He was. So was his sister.'

Of course she was. Elissa Jarvis would be up to anyone's requirements; she was an exceptionally beautiful girl.

Rowan kicked a rug off, remembered that later a cool breeze always sprang up and put it back again. She wondered if Elissa was having a restless night. Perhaps she was at the window, as she herself had been that first time, breathing in the pungent ginger air. Though probably she and Jonathan were talking long into the night, Jonathan rolling his bush cigarettes, telling her some of the tall stories of this tall state.

Would Elissa get up for breakfast, or would Nancy take it in? – Or would he? Calling 'Rise and shine' as he put down the tray, a tray with a steaming teapot and a dainty cup, thin toast, ginger preserve ... and a shoot of red flower.

Angry beyond all credence, angry with herself because she was angry, Rowan turned from the window and tried again to sleep. It was no use. Her resentment was eating into her. Why ... *why* had he made a rule, that ridiculous rule of circumspection, then suddenly change it to suit himself? For that must be the reason. It suited him.

Elissa suited him.

What do I care? Rowan said to the darkness. Why should I care? He's only the trustee.

'You were talking in your sleep last night,' said Nicholas over breakfast.

'Did you hear what I said?'

'No, I was too occupied with myself – with Miss Mary, to be exact. I've been estimating that that girl should be ready within the week.'

'Your sister—' began Rowan, feeling he should know that his sister had not slept at the stud.

'She won't be a scrap of help, but thank goodness I won't need help. The mare is in perfect condition, and' ... with boyish self-effacement ... 'I've always delivered pretty well. I want to do it by myself, Rowan. This first one has to be mine and mine alone.'

'Yes, Nicholas,' Rowan said quite fondly, for she believed she knew how he felt.

She stacked the dishes for Mrs. White, then walked along the track to Tom Thumb, looking up, as she always did, for the familiar skein of woodsmoke billowing from the black beast. Once the smoke escaped Eats' crooked chimney it changed its menacing appearance into a soft blue weave. She liked to think it was *her* smoke. So long as it wreathed upward, she felt proudly, I'm in business. She glanced triumphantly across at The Outlook, still standing virgin.

She was late this morning, and Barney was ready to leave.

'Fair only,' he reported, 'and so spaced I couldn't get all the cut lunches ready.'

'Don't worry, Barney, it mightn't be a busy morning.'

Rowan put on an apron . . . not one of Elissa's pretty offerings, she was keeping those for the times when business really got down . . . and started slicing the corned beef.

Her thoughts absorbed her. Had Elissa gone straight home without calling here first or was she still at Narganoo? If so, how long did she intend to stop there? . . . and how long did the trustee intend to waive that rule he had made?

It was not until she got to the end of the large loaf, which was quite a job, that it occurred to her that business was *very* moderate. In fact there was no business at all. Oh, well, that was how the cookie . . . in this instance the corned dog and pickle . . . crumbled. What you didn't get in the morning, you got in the afternoon, and if you didn't get it then, you got it at night.

Or . . . standing transfixed at a sight she had known she must see some day . . . you didn't get it at all.

For across the road, no need of any skeins of smoke because the ranges there were nice and clean and modern and electric, and like a fool she had forgotten, half a dozen trucks were pulled up. And not pulled up just to look, for The Outlook's doors were wide open, music breathed faintly across to her . . . and so did something that could be nothing else but steak.

The opposition had opened.

Wretchedly, Rowan went to the door and peered out. By now she had come to know a lot of her regulars, and she judged that three of the trucks at least were just that – or had been that.

Roy, Perce, Snow, she enumerated bitterly. She hoped the steak was only fit to take to a mat and squat down and gnaw as you called yourself Fido.

Still, in all fairness, she could not blame the hauliers. They lived a hard life, no one lived harder, and even if they came back to her, they still had to try out the new place, it was only human nature. And they were trying it.

The trouble was there was no provision for even a trial in Uncle Tom's will. If every haulier only patronized The Outlook just the once, and once was an impossible dream, it would still look bad on her account sheet.

She had known it was to come, but she had never felt she would take it so bitterly. Going back to the kitchen, she looked forlornly at her pile of sandwiches, waiting to be parcelled and stacked in the fridge.

At noon she had a mild flutter, but mild only. Also, every one of the customers took a long considering look at the new café . . . or considering, Rowan considered it.

To make it worse, if anything could have made it worse, during the afternoon cars pulled up . . . she had never really got over her yearning for a tea shop, for a clientele like those people obviously were . . . and customers went in. Later they emerged, looking well pleased. Sandwiches cut in fours, thought Rowan jealously, perhaps not the special layer cake I planned, but *cake*.

She made a cup of tea and let it get cold. She forgot to stoke the fire, then, remembering, made it so red-hot that the galvanized building, never the coolest spot, became a furnace.

She ran out and washed her hot face in the tin basin under the mango tree, wondering what the ablutions were like over there. She had had dreams of her own, and she would have carried them out, only she hadn't had the money nor the time. If you had the money, she thought, you always snatched the time. She saw a truck approaching and waited for it to go, as the others had, across the road. But it stayed this side, and Rowan rushed in and put on one of Elissa's pink aprons. Now she really had to try.

But the truck didn't want s. and e., just a box of matches.

'Got a rival,' the driver said, not even looking at Rowan or the apron, looking at The Outlook ... and no doubt marking it in his mind for trial on the way down south again.

Late in the afternoon Elissa came in.

'Jonathan put me off at the end of the road,' she said. 'I've had a wonderful morning. Ginger is certainly a fascinating thing.'

'Very fascinating.'

'We were shocked to see what had happened,' Elissa said sympathetically next. 'I mean, Rowan, you know it will happen, but it still comes as a surprise. Are your takings down, do you think?'

'As down as one box of matches.'

'Not *really*?'

'Near enough.'

'A rotten show. Still, as Jonathan said, it's not an end ... that is, not for you.'

'Then to whom is it an end?'

'Oh, darling, don't be so touchy. Jonathan and I talked hours last night. It got me out of myself, to think about someone instead of myself.'

'Like – Larry?' It came instinctively to Rowan's lips, and she had the satisfaction of seeing Elissa lose some of her good humour.

'How long did he stay?' she asked sharply.

'Oh, he didn't run away the moment he found you'd gone.'

'I don't know what you're talking about, Rowan.'

'I'm sorry, Elissa,' Rowan said insincerely. 'The gentleman who called at the stud last night left quite early. I think' ... again it was instinct that urged her ... 'he's in training. It could be that he's not just an arranging boss but a working boss as well. I mean of course the rodeo and the novice event. Did you think he looked a novice?'

'How should I know?' Elissa's voice had a high unnatural note, and Rowan could tell that her words had hit home. She could see the colour ebbing from Elissa, and she felt sorry if she had started something. Yet after all, why should everything be all right for Elissa, why shouldn't she suffer as well? Suffer? Now that was really overdoing it. All I did, Rowan thought, was lie and look at Nicholas's barns and wonder if Elissa was looking at the ginger crop. Suffer! She laughed.

'I'm glad you're amused, Rowan,' Elissa said coldly. She looked bleak and pinched all at once.

'Oh, I'm not,' Rowan said, 'I'm rock bottom.' She glanced to the door and beyond the door. 'But what can I do?'

'It doesn't really matter,' repeated Elissa. 'Jonathan said—' She must have seen a look on Rowan's face, for she left it at that.

The lack of trade continued into the evening. When Barney came Rowan showed him the sandwiches in stock and advised him not to cut any more.

'I'm sorry, Rowan,' Barney said awkwardly, looking around at the empty tables.

'I'm sorry for *you*, Barney,' Rowan proffered. 'This was your dream, wasn't it?'

He seemed embarrassed at first, then he shifted his weight to his other foot and said he supposed it was in a way.

'It did seem the sort of retirement business that would suit me,' he admitted.

'And suit Nancy?'

Barney went a brick red.

Barney, you don't have to have a prize for a girl.'

'Nancy's not that any more. Not a girl.'

'You still don't have to have it, whatever her age.'

'I do. I wouldn't ask any woman ... I mean, well, I wouldn't. Not without being able to say, "Well, here it is," if you know what I mean.'

'I don't.'

'All the same it's how I feel.'

'You are a stubborn old man.'

'We're what we are,' was all Barney would say.

'Nancy, too?'

'Look, it's all over. I knew that when Tom died before he could talk the caff over with me, come to terms. I'm used to it now. But you ... well, even though you knew the place over the road was coming it must still be a shock.'

'Yes,' admitted Rowan. 'I can never pick up today's loss, nor tomorrow's ... nor next week's. Even if I did come good again I can't get the figures I'm down up again, that is in sufficient time. I mean, probates have to be settled. Wills don't carry on for years. Also Jonathan Saxby is so – so—'

Barney nodded. 'Jonathan is always with the law,' he said proudly. 'No one has ever pointed a finger at Jonathan.'

'Very straight and narrow,' agreed Rowan, stringently, adding to herself, 'Except at times.' – Elissa times.

Angry with the way she was chewing over something that should be forgotten by now, she went off to the stud.

Business was no better the next day. A few *very* regular regulars remained faithful, but Rowan could see that they were curious to say the least, and from curiosity sprang the need to find out for yourself.

'Have to see what poison they're hitting you with over there,' breezed Sam.

From a steak and a bundle of sandwiches at noon ... 'no room across the road', which seemed to Rowan the ultimate barb ... up to tea-time there was not one customer. Then something was pulling up and she ran out eagerly.

It was the bus, the driver who first had brought her here, calling, 'Hi there, settled in? So you've the opposition as I said. Never mind, the truckies will soon see where their bread's buttered. Ho-ho!' As before he enjoyed his own play of words.

'Are you stopping?' she asked.

'Only to drop some mail. Is Redland you?'

'Yes.'

'Then sign the book, it's a parcel. I don't carry the letter mail, but I carry parcels. How are they doing across the road? What's the grub like? But then I don't suppose you'd know. Never mind, I'll try it myself and tell you. Better get on.'

Rowan watched him go. As on the day she had arrived there were no passengers, but then he had told her he picked them up further along, down this end was always a loss, but he had to do it because of the timetable.

She did not think about the parcel, and if she had she would have dismissed it as something the girls had sent on from the hostel. Even when Barney arrived and handed it to her from the kitchen table where she had flung then promptly forgotten it she still did not think about it. She never thought about it as she walked to the stud.

She had supper with Nicholas and Elissa, talked, listened to records, then went along to her room. The parcel now was where she had tossed it on the bed. Something she had sent for while she was still in London, she decided, a catalogue or so. The girls needn't have bothered to re-direct it.

She was almost inclined to leave it. Not that she was

tired, she had done nothing to make her tired, she was simply disinclined. However, she did snap the string, and then she removed another protective sheet of paper. Very carefully wrapped, she thought, unfolding it, then saw why. Bibles at most times are finely presented, and her mother's was old as well as fragile.

Sitting down on the bed, she opened it up. There, in her mother's delicate writing, on the front page was the record of the family. What a shame this sort of thing was not done much now! She glanced through it, wondering why she had never noticed before the brackets beside her mother's name. She read Selina Thumb (n. Walters). N. would be née, she knew now.

She was closing the Bible again when something caught her eye. She took the Bible up.

Six girls and a boy, her mother had told her, all producing a chick apiece, except Thomas. Yet—

Mary . . . . . . Loris
Olga . . . . . . Jessica
Agnes . . . . . . Gladwyn
Dora . . . . . . Hal
Frances . . . . . . Pearce
Selina (n. Walters) . . . . . . Rowan
Then:
Thomas. By adoption: Jonathan Saxby.

Thomas. By adoption. Jonathan Saxby. So there *were* six others as Pearce had said.

But why hadn't Jonathan said?

She remembered other things that Pearce had hinted. She remembered him warning her not to expect any preferential treatment from the trustee. Of course she would receive no preferential treatment when he was one of the family, *one of the rest of the family who stood to inherit if she did not succeed.*

How had Uncle Tom come to adopt a child? Had he

154

been married? She had thought you had to be married to take over the care of a minor.

Then it occurred to her, and she was not aware she was clutching at it eagerly, that a trustee could not inherit, which ruled Jonathan out. She did not mind Jonathan being just, but she could not bear the thought of Jonathan being just ... *for a purpose*. She was sure she had read somewhere that being a trustee ruled being a beneficiary as well right out.

She was not aware she was running down the hall and knocking on Nicholas's door until Nicholas said: 'What is it, a fire?'

'Just – just a puzzle.'

'Crossword?'

'Something like that. Nicholas, can a trustee of a will be included in the will?' Answering before he could, she said, 'I'm sure he can't.'

'You're thinking of a witness, Rowan. A trustee can benefit. Is witness what you wanted?'

'I think so. Yes. Thank you, Nicholas. Sorry to disturb you. It was just one of those things.'

'I know. They nag at you. I've been looking up the calendar, and Miss Mary's date is nagging me.'

'Poor Nicholas!' But as she walked back to her room Rowan was thinking, Poor me. Poor me to have been such a blind fool as to have swallowed Jonathan's self-righteousness. All the time, even when he was sympathetically telling me about the new motorway and what a goldmine the café could be, he was aware of this. Why, otherwise, would he have been so angry every time I mentioned that I'd sent for the family records? He knew whatever happened that he and the other five were to benefit, because he had the final say, but where they made no secret about it, he did. He's a sneaking, low-down, unprincipled user of people; he used Uncle

Thomas, and now he's used me. Even if by some miracle I had succeeded with the café, succeeded beyond the greatest expectation, I would still have been passed over. Money is a remarkable thing, especially money like that.

No wonder he spoke like he did that day about Uncle Tom Thumb! 'Thumb,' he had said, 'I would have given the best years of my life for such a name.' Well, he hadn't had to waste time, waste those years, but the result would be the same.

Yet perhaps she was letting her suppositions run away with her. *Be fair*, she said sternly. You never did read the will, you just half-listened to Mr. Purkiss, your mind was full of little cafés serving cinnamon toast. Why, even when he started to read out the alternative beneficiaries you stopped him and recited them yourself. At least you believed you did.

And perhaps you did. Perhaps when it came to it, Uncle Thomas only wrote down the blood relations, having decided that since one non-blood inheritor had not succeeded he wouldn't waste time with a second. Perhaps Jonathan Saxby was never included, perhaps step-cousin Pearce had only been trying to scare me out.

There was only one way to discover the truth, and Rowan knew it. She could not go to Jonathan and say, 'Are you or are you not a possible inheritor?' and she would never ask a step-cousin.

She knew that wills could be read, and since this one had been made in Australia that it could be read here. Read not so far away, either. Only as far as Brisbane. I'll go tomorrow, she knew. I have to find out.

In the morning when Elissa came to the café she asked her to mind the shop, though it was the most ludicrous thing she had ever asked, for there was no business to mind.

'Of course. Taking off?'

'Yes. Brisbane.'

'What?'

'Brisbane. Just there and back.'

'What for?'

'I didn't ask why you went, Elissa.'

'Sorry, but you don't seem a feckless type like I am. If it's shopping you're after, let's both go up to—'

'I'm going to Brisbane. I'm going to hitch a ride.'

'After what you said to me?' Rowan shrugged. 'Also,' pointed out Elissa, 'from whom?' That made sense; there was not one customer, up or down, at Eats.

'From someone across the road,' said Rowan, and picking up her bag, she crossed.

She had no trouble. After all she was twenty-two and would pass, she thought bitterly. The driver was manageably amorous, and even quite nice. He was on a short haul, and said he could bring her back tonight.

It didn't take long once she got into the city, and none of it was any trouble. She found the appropriate office, stated her case to see the copy, and it was brought out.

'. . . to my niece, Rowan Redland, a young woman I have never met . . .'

She skipped that.

She skipped . . . '. . . but only if she carries on the said estate . . .'

She skipped . . . '. . . the judge of this to be my old friend and trustee Jonathan Saxby . . .' (For a moment she remembered how she had thought Jonathan Saxby would be a senior citizen with a leaning to seedcake.)

Then she came to what she had come for.

Mr. Purkiss had said, 'There now follows a list of names,' and she had broken in, 'Loris, Jessica, Gladwyn, Hal and Pearce.'

Only there was one more. The will clearly said so.

After Pearce there came Jonathan Saxby.

So he would benefit by her failure!

'Thank you,' she said, and went out.

She met the haulier as arranged, and he complained that she was not as good company going back as she had been coming.

'I'm sorry.' She did feel sorry, she felt sorry for everyone. And herself.

She got out at Eats, watching unmoved as the truckie crossed to The Outlook, then went in, expecting to see Barney or Elissa.

Jonathan waited there.

'The other two have gone,' he said. 'No need to stay open tonight ... any night. Where in Betsy have you been?'

'Brisbane.'

'Elissa said so, but I wouldn't believe her.'

'Well, that's where I went.'

'If you had wanted anything you should have told me.'

'What I wanted you wouldn't have got me.'

'Oh, if it was feminine things you could have written it down.'

'Not this thing,' she said.

'Very secretive, aren't you?'

'Yes. Like you.'

'And what do you mean by that?'

'I think you know, Mr. Saxby, *ward of Thomas Thumb.*'

He had turned away from her, apparently irritated by her behaviour, but now he whirled round.

'So,' he said. 'That's what it's all about.'

'Yes.'

'Your records arrived.'

'Yes.'

'You went down to Brisbane to check something.'

'Yes.'

'Because you believed that I—'

'Yes.'

'And you found out.'

'Yes.'

'And your finding, Miss Redland?'

'Yes, yes, yes!' She fairly screamed it at him.

He had come to her. 'Quieten down. We've no trade, but at least we have no panic. Another outburst like that and someone will call the police.' He waited a moment. 'You've found out that you have another cousin, haven't you, or wasn't cousin the name you then allotted me?'

'It wasn't,' she said grimly.

'You found out that I stood, with the others, to benefit if you couldn't make the grade?'

Again she said, but in a disciplined voice now: 'Yes.'

'So immediately you saw the light ... *your* light. I was the ugly go-between, the one who really fixed it that you went down in flames.'

For answer she flung, 'Why don't you go over the road where you should be, Mr. Saxby?'

'Because,' he said, 'I want to stay here and shake every breath out of your body. Oh, I know I've shaken before, but this time I want to fix you properly, Rowan Redland.'

'And kiss me afterwards in case by some mistake I do win and you can still be on both sides?'

For a moment she thought he *was* going to shake her, and remembering last time she half-stepped back.

Then he said quietly, 'No. Oh, no, Rowan. Like your trade, that's all gone.' He turned and went out.

What had gone? And why hadn't she ever suspected it was there ... if it had been there? For a thing to be gone, it must have existed. Had it existed?

She heard the car go and felt the tears burning down her cheeks. Because, she knew, it *did* exist . . . for me. I think I knew it that first moment he came out with a pencil behind his ear and said: 'Who's standing the sandwiches?'

He stood there . . . just there . . . and he – he was the one.

Like the girls used to say with the stale sandwich and the dud cake, I always made a wrong choice.

CHAPTER TEN

THE next morning Elissa said sympathetically to Rowan, 'You look bowled out, darling. By Jonathan? Well, you did ask for it, taking off like that.'

They were still at the breakfast table. What was the good of hurrying to open a shop that had no customers?

'You must have had a reason for that sudden trip south,' persisted Elissa.

Rowan got up, saying she better make an appearance if nothing else at Tom Thumb. As she walked listlessly down the track she decided it was better, anyway, than being probed by Elissa.

Barney had left for the cut, but the door was not locked. Who would steal a big black beast of a stove or plates that even a cement motorway would not have challenged? He had left a note for Rowan, and it was typical of straight-to-the-point Barney. It said simply: 'Nothing doing.'

It seemed impossible that only a week ago this place had hummed with activity. Undoubtedly a lot of customers would come back, human nature being what it was, people being kind, faithful to old friends, to familiar corners, but to produce a satisfactory profit and loss sheet, satisfactory for the terms of a will, it had to be AS GOOD. Uncharitably Rowan wondered if Jonathan had suggested that AS GOOD term to Uncle Tom; it was the kind of sly thing he would do. She mightn't care for her step-cousins, but at least their rivalry was direct, not hidden in smooth subtleties and polite half-truths.

Thinking of her step-cousins must have been an omen, for Pearce walked in.

'Good morning, Rowan.'

'Good morning.'

'Business as usual?'

'Not as usual.'

'But as usual,' he pointed out, 'as the last few days.'

'If you've come to gloat . . .' she began.

'My dear girl, nothing could be further from my mind.'

'Then what have you come for? A loan of something?'

He looked aghast, and glancing around, she did not wonder. Empty like this, and no reassuring if overheating fire, it seemed more depressing than ever.

'Actually I came because I'm not happy about you.'

'It's a little late, isn't it?'

'Oh, come now, Rowan, you must admit that in our shoes you would have done the same yourself.'

'Perhaps,' she nodded wearily, 'especially when I knew about the new motorway.'

'Oh, so you've heard.'

'I've been told.' She paused. 'By Mr. Saxby.'

'Yes, I suppose he could afford to do that, knowing it could make no difference to the final issue. The whole thing has been most unfortunate. If only Uncle Thomas had made a proper will in the first place!'

Something nagged at Rowan . . . then she remembered it.

'There was a will before this one, wasn't there?' She looked so unwaveringly at Pearce that he turned his own glance away.

'Well – maybe.' He did not linger on the subject. 'But the important thing is that this one is now the order of the day. By any chance did you check it up, my dear?'

'I think you saw me leave yesterday.'

'So you did go. Then you would see how Jonathan

Saxby stands to benefit, too.'

'I saw. Was there anything you wanted?'

This time Pearce did not look at the café aghast, instead he looked at Rowan admiringly.

'I don't know if you're aware of it, but I'm the only one of your step-cousins not married.'

'Jonathan . . .' His name came out before she realized it.

Pearce made a gesture of impatience. 'That's so, but I hardly call him a cousin.'

'I'm not myself.'

'I *know*,' said Pearce, moving forward, 'and I'm very glad. You're extremely attractive, Rowan. No wonder all our mothers were jealous of the little girl who came with Grandfather's second marriage.' He smiled fatuously at Rowan.

'You're also,' he went on before she could comment, 'a long way from home, aren't you? Do you ever get lonely, Rowan?'

'No.'

'I suppose you miss the old life?'

'I like it here.'

'Well' . . . a step nearer . . . 'there could be a way of remaining. Have you thought of that?'

'A lot. Only when you opened up it was no use thinking any more.'

'But, Rowan, you said you didn't blame us.'

'I don't, but I still don't have to love you.'

'Not the girls, perhaps. Not Hal. But—' He looked inquiringly at Rowan. 'I'm a deal younger than the others,' he said, 'and quite well-established even without what lies ahead.' He nodded back to The Outlook . . . and as he nodded three more trucks pulled up.

'Do you always propose like this?' asked Rowan boldly.

'It's the first time I've ever proposed in my life.'

'Then it will be the first time you've been refused.'

'Rowan, my dear—'

'You heard the lady. She's refused.' It was Jonathan, who had come silently into Tom Thumb, and he was moving across to Pearce.

Pearce stepped back ... after all, Jonathan was very large. But he could not resist saying, 'At least I had a name to offer her.' He didn't quite finish. The last few words came in mid-air as Jonathan impelled him out.

'Barbarian,' Rowan said, and she said it of the trustee, for she was even more disgusted with Jonathan's behaviour than Pearce's oiliness.

'Often we're considered the barbarian state up here,' he came back. 'What did you expect me to do?'

'Ignoring him would have been better.'

'Perhaps. But that sort of gibe went out in the Victorian era. Besides' ... without emotion ... 'it isn't true.'

'You said once you'd give your best years to have been a Thumb.'

'That's true. Want to hear the story?'

'I think,' said Rowan coldly, 'I've had my surfeit of stories.'

'Rowan ... about last night ...'

'I've also,' she said, 'had a surfeit of you. You may be the trusteee, my fate at one time may have depended on you, or so I believed, not knowing that a pre-decision had been made, but it doesn't mean I still have to kow-tow to you, say yes, sir, no, sir—'

'Three bags full,' he finished wearily. 'All right, have it your way.' He turned and went out.

Several trucks did pull in, after all. One because they were filled up over the road and the driver had a time clause hanging over him, and the other because last time

164

he had left his tobacco pouch here.

Late in the morning Elissa came along. She was the old Elissa, restless, irritable, driven by some thought that only she knew. She picked up things, put them down again. One of the things she picked up was the folder of rodeo tickets. She re-read them, then replaced them.

Rowan made tea and opened a packet of sandwiches that were still piled up in the fridge. 'I can't waste food,' she offered apologetically.

'No,' agreed Elissa, uninterested.

They sat there without talking, both intent on their own concerns, and because of their silence the impact was even louder.

'What in heaven is that?' Elissa sat up, startled . . . but Rowan already had got to her feet.

She was out of Eats and racing down the motorway, dreading what she could see, but knowing that she must face up to it whatever it was, however awful, if she wanted to help.

Around the bend the cause of the violent noise met her horrified gaze. Two trucks had collided, one had gone up the bordering bank and the other had turned right over. Their occupants, considerably more than the drivers and offsiders, so there must have been pick-ups in the back of each lorry, were strewn across the highway. Rowan counted at least ten casualties . . . at least she hoped that casualties were all they were. Some were moaning. One was trying to untangle a tangled leg. One was holding his head. One seemed to lie horribly still.

She was aware that Elissa was now with her. She wondered how the girl would react, because so far Elissa had only shown a very flippant front. So long, she thought, steeling herself to move forward, as she doesn't panic.

But – 'I've rung Nicholas,' Elissa said, 'I've rung Jonathan. Jonathan is contacting police, ambulance, doctors, hospital.' She stepped forward with Rowan.

The next hour went as though it was a minute, and yet, realized Rowan proudly, everything was done in its proper way. The police sealed off the motorway. The doctors ... and Nicholas ... sorted out the casualties (thank heaven it was only that), then sent the worst ones off in the ambulance. Back in Tom Thumb the lesser fractures, sprains and shocks were attended to, then they, too, were taken off by car.

In an almost incredibly short time it was all over. The road was cleared, the motorway opened up again. Jonathan had piled his car with a broken toe, a twisted wrist, a slight shock that had received hot sugared tea and an extra rug, and taken them off.

Nicholas, needed no more, had gone back to the stud where Miss Mary might need him ... and Elissa said, 'Phew!' and sat down and looked at Rowan.

'You were wonderful, Elissa,' Rowan said warmly.

'You were yourself.'

'Yes, but ... well ...'

'You didn't expect it of me?' Elissa shrugged.

Rowan said frankly, thinking how the accident had loosened up everything so that she could speak more directly: 'No.'

'But then you don't know me.'

Rowan replied, thinking now that even Nicholas did not know his sister: 'Does anyone?'

'Yes. One.'

'Who, Elissa?'

'He knows me, and I ... I ...' She got up from the chair into which she had flopped so exhaustedly and began pacing the room in the old Elissa way. 'Rowan,' she said miserably, 'this thing just now has shattered me.'

'That's aftermath, Elissa.'

'*Not* the accident ... I mean not the actuality of it ...

but – well, the possibility of it. Of – of disaster.'

'You mean in the midst of life we are in death.'

'*Don't!*' Elissa turned almost desperately to Rowan. Presently she said more quietly, 'All those pick-ups were hitching a ride to the rodeo.'

'Yes, I heard them say so.'

Another pause, then:

'Rowan, I have to go.'

'Go?'

'Go there as well – to the rodeo. I said I wouldn't, but I have to. Will you take me?'

'What, Elissa?' queried Rowan.

'Don't ask why, just please drive me, because . . . well, I don't think I can drive myself.'

'But, Elissa—'

'Please do it, Rowan. Please!'

Rowan looked at her a searching minute, recognized an intense urgency, then got up, closed the shop, said, 'Come on, then, I only hope I can manage the car, and I only hope we find the way.'

'Brudwick lies west of a turn-off twenty miles up and it's another thirty miles from the road sign. A very clear sign. You see' . . . with a funny little laugh . . . 'I know all the details.'

'Are you all right, Elissa?' Rowan asked with concern.

'Yes.' Then Elissa said oddly, or oddly it sounded to Rowan: '*At last.*'

There was no looking at the scenery today. Rowan concentrated on the unfamiliar gears of a car she had never driven and Elissa sat huddled and unspeaking. She was alert, though, and warned Rowan of the approaching turn-off before it came into sight.

'You've been here before?'

'Yes.'

'Like to tell me, Elissa? Oh, not the full story, but—'

'I can't.' Elissa's teeth were actually chattering; she was in a highly nervous state. Rowan, concerned, went to pull up, but at once the girl put out a trembling hand. 'Just keep going, Rowan, for heaven's sake.'

Rowan drove on.

Soon she saw that they were not the only travellers to Brudwick, and she remembered one of the men . . . Nicholas? Jonathan? . . . saying that western shows were part of living up here. She reduced her speed, aware of Elissa's impatient anxiety, but there was nothing else for it but to join the long ribbon of traffic. Brudwick, when they reached it, was not so large as Round Corner, yet still a substantial country town. The rodeo was in the shire oval, and the usual procession had been staged in the morning, as well as the open events. This, anyway, was what the girls were told as they pushed their way to the corral where the afternoon's big attraction, the Novice, was to be staged.

Now Elissa was looking around her desperately. 'I have to stop him,' she said.

Rowan did not ask whom, she simply nodded and let the girl lead the way.

Elissa was hurrying to the back of the corral, seeking out different outfits, the carvans serving them. She went urgently up to each, each time turning away.

'Is it the Boys you're after, Elissa?' Rowan took a chance and asked directly.

'Yes.'

'. . . Larry?'

'Yes.'

'You're frightened he'll—'

'I'm frightened he's really going on with it, with his entry. His name was down on the programme. I saw it days ago.'

'And what are you actually frightened of, darling?'

'Him. Doing something like this. Because ... well, because he can't. Because' ... wretchedly ... 'I taunted him.'

'Elissa—' Rowan began.

'Oh, I can't tell you now. I have to find him, stop him.' A break in her voice. 'Tell him.'

'Tell him what? I mean, Elissa, when a man has gone this far—'

'Tell him ... how I feel. Tell him that I ... that I ... Oh, help me, Rowan!' again Elissa appealed. 'Help me, please!'

'There's the outfit now.' Rowan had glimpsed the grey, and, recognizing the pony, looked around and recognized some of the men.

Elissa raced forward. Rowan heard her incoherent voice and wondered if she was making any sense. She must have, though, for one of them ... Trev? Dick? ... said, 'But he'll be next in. It would be no use. It would be too late.'

There was the roar of the crowd as yet another competitor was released from his small waiting space, and once again (in Rowan's mind) Rowan saw the swirl of flying hooves as a horse pig-rooted, kicked, threw and heaved in the effort to throw his rider.

She did not know that Elissa was seeing it, too, *but not in her mind*, until she realized that the girl had pushed away from her, had pushed through the crowd.

She followed just in time to see the corral attendants leaping for the rails. And to see Larry thrown to the ground.

After that everything seemed to happen like the flashing mirrors and facets of a kaleidoscope. Elissa was in the arena and the horse was being caught and taken away. A stretcher was being brought in, and the bearers

169

were trying to persuade Elissa to get up from the ground so that they could lift Larry up to be attended. Elissa still crouched there, the man's head on her lap.

'Perhaps I can do something.' Rowan climbed over and went in. 'Elissa darling—' she appealed.

Elissa looked up and her eyes were dull.

'Is he—' she asked. 'Rowan, is he—'

'No, nothing like that. But certainly dazed. Possibly concussed. Elissa, you must let these men take over.'

Rowan doubted if she would have even listened to her, let alone heed her, had not at that moment the man opened his eyes and looked fully at Elissa.

'Yes,' he said, 'do that.'

The girl sat on a moment, then she let the attendants slide a cushion to where the head had rested against her, then slide Larry on to a stretcher. She let Rowan help her up, take her arm, lead her out.

'He isn't dead, is he?'

'Darling, he's very alive.'

'He spoke to me, didn't he?'

'Yes, he asked you to let the ambulance men take over.'

'He'll be all right, won't he?'

'Of course, Elissa.'

'Because you see' . . . Elissa swallowed hard . . . 'I'm his wife.'

It was an hour afterwards and in the base hospital at Brudwick. Larry had been X-rayed, then the negative result permitting it been administered a sedative and left to rest.

'When he wakes up and not before,' the doctor had stipulated, 'you can see your husband, Mrs. Mason.'

'Mrs. Mason.' Elissa Jarvis was Elissa Mason. 'Does Nicholas—' began Rowan.

'No,' intercepted Elissa, 'Nicholas doesn't know I'm married, Rowan.'

The little waiting room was empty. Rowan guessed it would be rather like Christmas, no one got sick at Christmas, not in London anyway, that is, unless . . . unhappily . . . they could not help it. Up here in Brudwick evidently no one got sick on a rodeo day. The girls had the place to themselves.

'No, Nicholas doesn't know,' repeated Elissa. 'No one knows except Larry and me.' A tight little laugh. 'The partners in the contract. We're both impetuous people, one of a sort really, we should have made a go of it. When Larry proposed out of the blue to me I simply answered Yes.' A pause. 'We went that afternoon.' Her eyes dreamed.

'How long did it—'

'Did it last? Practically as long as it took to do. And that was my fault. I've always been spoiled, Rowan, hopelessly, rottenly spoiled. Nicholas is quite a few years older than I am, and when our parents died he took me over, but his idea of taking me over was giving me anything I desired. He just couldn't deny me, and it had unforunate results.'

'Oh, Elissa!'

'That's true. I was a brat. I had a lot of silly affairs, but all the same when I met Larry, I knew. I mean you do know, don't you?'

'Yes,' Rowan said, 'you know.'

'He asked me, and I agreed, and I thought that was all there was to it. Only . . .' Elissa's voice trailed off.

'Only there was more?' helped Rowan.

'A lot more,' Elissa said.

'Larry had been passed on his father's entrepreneur business. Do you know what that means?'

'One who undertakes an enterprise, a kind of contractor.'

'Yes. Old Mr. Mason had a string of these commitments, ranging from ballet to Shakespeare to – well, to this.' She spread her hands. 'On his death Larry took them over. It's very lucrative, in fact a goldmine.'

She was quiet a while, and Rowan did not worry her.

'You don't know me,' she said presently, 'I really have a very bad nature.'

'Darling—'

'No, Rowan, I *have*. I just have to be contra, somehow. Nicholas always said it was the shock of Mum and Dad at my immature, vulnerable age, but Nicholas has always been kind.'

'Yes, Elissa?'

'The ballet and the Shakespeare were all right, but when I learned about the Boys, of the Western Outfit, I was insulting, Rowan, terribly insulting ... I can be ... and Larry was hurt. I should have called a halt when I saw how he was taking it, but a demon got into me, and I went on ... and on. I'm a good horsewoman – you've seen that. Another of Nicholas's indulgences. He stood me the best of teachers. I knew that I was better than Larry ever would be – if that mattered.'

'It doesn't,' said Rowan softly.

'I know. Oh, I know that. *Now*.'

'I jeered at the idea of an indifferent horseman like Larry managing a Western troupe like this, and – well, it went on from there. It was a hideous quarrel, as hideous as you can think. And it was entirely my fault. I packed up straight away and went home to Nicholas.'

'Didn't he question you about leaving your husband? Didn't he reason with you?'

'He didn't know. I told you. It was done in an impetuous rush, and the awful, the hideous quarrel occurred in a week. Previously we had inherited the property from a distant relative ... it had meant little to me then, but when Nicholas unfolded his plans, I asked eagerly if I could come, too. I -- I said I was finished with a love affair I had grown tired of, that perhaps in the north I could find new interests. Nicholas took me up at once, except that he took me up a little too much' ... a rueful laugh ... 'even made matrimonial plans. I went along with him to the degree of trying to have fun, but all the time I knew it was no use, Rowan. Because' ... softly now ... 'you can arrange your life, but you can't arrange your heart.'

'You still love Larry?'

'I never stopped loving him. I simply rebelled from the sudden change from utter freedom to – well, I chose to consider it bondage. Though that wasn't true. It wasn't that Larry ever wanted me to go his way, he wanted us to meet on the same ground, but I accused him of demanding compliance.'

'Yes,' smiled Rowan, 'but your word was obedience, you said all men wanted obedience.'

'I said a lot of things,' Elissa cried.

'Well, it's all over, darling. He's unhurt, it's just a matter of waiting.'

'For what?'

Almost as if in answer a nurse came in. 'Mrs. Mason?'

Elissa jumped up. 'Yes?'

'Can you come? No, don't look alarmed, he's fine. I'm sorry' ... to Rowan ... 'but he only asked for his wife.'

'Of course,' Rowan said, and gave Elissa a little smile.

She sat on for a long time. Whatever was being settled in there was being settled thoroughly.

Then the nurse came in again.

'I hope you don't mind once more, but Mrs. Mason was

thinking that perhaps you'd like to leave without her. They're a very young and very devoted couple, aren't they?'

'Yes,' Rowan agreed faintly.

'She said you may be inconvenienced, so not to wait for her, to take the car. She can put up locally. For that matter we can accommodate her here.'

'Yes,' Rowan agreed again.

She did not go in to say good-bye . . . good luck . . . to Elissa, she simply went across to the parking area, but as she passed a window she saw two heads together, and she knew that good luck was not needed. Not there.

Absurdly happy, she ran across to the Jarvis car, and started off.

She could not have told at what juncture of her journey down she first noticed the long streaks of high cirrus like the flowing tails and manes of wild horses galloping full speed across a sky . . . 'Mares' tails', she knew they were called . . . but she did know that soon afterwards, alarmingly soon, the cirrus had merged into a threatening bank of fast-building dense black cloud.

Almost within minutes . . . *seconds* . . . the cloud filled the entire sky.

At once the wind struck.

CHAPTER ELEVEN

SHE seemed to be alone on the motorway, a glance in the rear vision mirror showed no vehicle behind her, there was no car in front. Probably everyone else had read the message of those massing clouds and sought shelter. She would have sought it, too, but this particular stretch of the bitumen was a lonely one, so the only thing to do was to keep on until something fairly protected offered refuge.

It was raining, but you could not have said that rain fell, because the gale was blowing the drops almost horizontally. They slashed against the side of the car. Sometimes the wind slightly lifted the car, but fortunately she was neither going into the wind nor being swept by it. At this stage the slight tangent at which the car met the onslaught helped somewhat.

At one time the road had a full view of the sea, that lovely millpond where the Barrier Reef islands lay embroidered in paisley colours on shining silk. But there were no paisleys now, no embroideries, no silk, instead rolling, monstrous water in cruel charcoal grey.

A particularly strong gust really lifted the car, and Rowan thought: I must do something. I can't go on like this.

She toyed with the idea of turning into the bush now rimming the road to the west, of trying to find a space between the dense trees. Trees could fall, but it would be bad luck if one fell where she placed the car, and at least she would not be lifted sickeningly up as she had been lifted just now. She watched for an opening, saw one, and slid in.

At once she knew she had made a mistake. She had imagined the noise element would be reduced. It wasn't, it was magnified a hundredfold, for besides the wind demons there was the roar of the protesting branches, the cries of the tormented leaves. When a deafening crash occurred somewhere near her, she knew a tree had fallen, and that this was no place for her. But when she tried to get out again, she saw that part of the fallen tree had entrapped her, there was no escaping the way she had come in. She ventured outside the car to see if there was a space to reverse, but she was trapped in as close and as contained a corner as though she had been fitted there.

Now she did not know what to do; to remain here was terrifying, yet she was afraid to return to the road. She stood there uncertainly till another crashing tree somewhere in the forest made up her mind, and, not waiting to take her things from the car seat, in fact too frightened to remain a moment longer, she raced out to the highway again, and, keeping to the rim in the hope that it afforded a measure of protection, she ran.

She was soaked within minutes. There was no escaping that fierce horizontal rain. She was practically blind as well, whipped-up spray from the sea had collected into a grey veil and made it an obscure world.

Her heart was protesting painfully, but she still kept running, she knew she could not keep it up, there were miles yet to go, but she could not remain still, there was no place to stand. Perhaps she should have stopped with the car . . . Nicholas's car. She felt guilty over that. But if anything was going to happen to it she could not prevent it. Also, she could not bring herself to go back.

If only some truck would come along, one of those big haulage trailers that could withstand a blast!

None came.

The wind was increasing. She could tell that by the

writing branches of the bordering trees that instead of just dropping their twigs and sticks to the ground now were flinging whole arms of them on the motorway. At one particularly violent blast even the bordering gravel was lifted, then thrown down again. The noise was thunderous. The wind shrieked and roared as it plunged and soared.

Then, through the dense grey, she saw something coming at her. At first she thought it was a house, a house lifted bodily by the wind and driven along the bitumen. Then, with relief, she saw that it was a truck. No trailer attached to anchor it down further, but a very substantial vehicle, and a heavy duty one. It had on its fog lights to cut the obscurity, and that was what had made her think of a house, a house with a yellow front beacon.

A horn's piercing warning, savagely applied by an angry finger, from the way it cut stridently through the noise, made her realize she was in the truck's way, and she leapt aside. At once the truck stopped, the cabin door opened, someone jumped out.

'You fool, you utter little damn fool, did you want me to drive over you?'

'I wanted you to see me.'

'I saw you ... heaven knows how I did from the way I've been straining my eyes looking for a glimpse of you, of the car ... and where is the car? No, don't answer. Get in.'

'Yes, Jonathan,' Rowan said.

Once in the cabin, it was a little better, though very little better.

'We better get going,' Jonathan said grimly.

'But in a heavy vehicle like this—'

'I've known heavy vehicles like this tossed around like leaves. Now where will I turn?' He drove up the motorway for a while, then found a spot. Meanwhile she began to tell him wretchedly about Nicholas's car, but he stopped her half-way.

'Forget it for now. At least you're not in it.'

'But if a tree falls on it . . .'

'Then it'll be finished, won't it?' As she did not answer, 'Look, it's only a car.'

All right for you, she thought, in your comfortable position, but how could *I* replace Nicholas's car?

'Rowan, for heaven's sake, we're not out of it yet ourselves,' he shouted, and, having turned, he began to drive as fast as the wind and the obscurity would permit back along the road.

'Are we going to Narganoo?' she asked.

'No, I'm taking you along to the café, Miss Redland, or would you prefer the stud, up the steps, right to the front door? What do you think?'

'Jonathan, don't shout at me like that. I only asked because I don't understand.'

'Then understand this: in weather like this you don't say where are you going, you just go. Actually what I have in mind is a rise between here and the next milepost. I think I can get behind it, I think I recall a rough track. We can shelter there.'

'Stay in the truck?'

'You can stay underneath it if you like.'

'Jonathan!'

'Well, don't be such a damn idiot. At any moment now it's going to break.'

'Going to break? But – but isn't this it?'

'A foretaste only.' He was pushing the truck to its utmost. 'If you could analyse it, you would see that the gale is blowing in a clockwise curve, but after a while the winds change to carrying arcs, and then that's it. Places already weakened by the first blast simply can't stand the change of attack. Havoc sets in. If we can weather that variation in the shelter behind the hill, we can take the opportunity of the calm, or the eye, or the core, as it's alternatively called, that will follow after, to get home.'

'You — you mean there'll be more yet?' Rowan asked, aghast.

'A lot more. Melinda ... as this one is to be called ... will quite possibly bring along a sister. Let's hope she's a little sister. Hold on, Rowan, this is the rise I saw where we're going to weather out the first attack.'

'The *first* attack!' Rowan groaned.

It was a bumpy, rutted way, barely a way at all, but where the hill rose to its highest level, Jonathan drove the truck into the base, and there they waited.

It was a nightmare experience, and yet for all the increased ferocity ... yes, Rowan learned, that savage wind she had known on the road could increase its ferocity ... she was not afraid as before. Not because of the protection of the large truck with its sheltering cabin, not because of the rise breaking the impact, but because Jonathan was there.

'Where did you get the truck?' she asked during a lull.

'It's mine, of course. What do you think I do, consign my products by car?'

'How did you know to come for me?'

'Elissa had rung Nicholas to tell her story, and she said she was not coming back tonight, that you would bring the car. Luckily Nicholas had the good sense, even though he's a southerner and not used to our weather, to read the signs in the sky. He promptly rang me.'

'And you came out for me.'

'It looks like it, doesn't it?' he said.

'Jonathan, I'm sorry.'

'Just sit tight, girl, a really good blow is coming. It always does after a breathing space.'

She sat tight, heard the roar, but, oddly, did not think much about it now. When it stopped, she saw that Jonathan was getting ready to move out.

'Isn't it just another lull?'

'It's a lull, but not just another one. It's that calm, eye, core. Now we race home.'

Race they did. Jonathan put his foot right down on the accelerator and they drove as fast, Rowan thought, as the demons of wind had driven.

They turned in at Narganoo.

They could not get there entirely. After three-quarters of the way a blown tree blocked the track.

'Out!' called Jonathan, and not waiting for her to comply, he fairly pulled her out. Together they ran the last half mile to the house. Nancy, watching for them, opened the door, then slammed it again.

Almost at once Melissa, Melinda's sister, broke.

'Big sister or little sister?' asked Rowan, crossing to the window where Jonathan was standing to look out as well on the whipped countryside.

He judged for a moment, then said, 'A little sister, I'd say, and thank heaven for that. But don't go getting any ideas, Rowan. You'll be here for the night, possibly tomorrow night as well.'

'The wind doesn't sound at all high here.'

'We're exceptionally well protected at Narganoo. The first Rays chose it with care.'

Rays? Rowan wondered, but she did not follow it up. She said, 'Also, we wouldn't get the full impact as on the actual coast.'

'Perhaps not. They'll be a shambles there, but the hill won't go scot free. I'll be all right, the ginger isn't a tall enough crop. Also I've already harvested, thank heaven. But the cane will get it, it will be tangled into a diabolical mess. Also, all the Macadamia nuts will be shaken out of the trees. However, it was always a matter of picking them up.'

'What's Melissa called? I mean weather-wise? Is she also a cyclone?'

'A secondary satellite cyclone only, and she won't be so fierce as Melinda, but more persistent. These younger sisters are inclined to sulk because they have to take second place, to indulge in fretful squalls. So you may as well relax, girl, you won't be leaving for hours.'

Nancy brought in tea, and they sat in the comfort of the large lounge, where Jonathan had actually lit a fire for the look of it since it was not even chilly, but the burning log, crackling reassuringly, settling down in its crimson embers, made the room a cheerful place. Rowan found herself quite enjoying her first cyclone, and she said so.

'Yes, it's cosy enough here, but some poor devils ...' Jonathan sighed.

He told her how further up the coast as soon as the radar cyclone warning station gave the word, experienced people began to prepare.

'How could one prepare? I mean you can't stop it.'

'If you know you're in the target area, and these days they can tell you right to the eye, or core, you evacuate, then billet your family.' He glanced affectionately at Nancy. 'I know someone who does a deal of advance cooking when she hears, just in case.'

They talked on till dark ... dark by time only, it had been near enough to dark ever since the winds had struck ... then they went to bed, Rowan to her first room again, the room that looked out on the ginger, though no use to open a window and snatch a breath tonight, for the ginger would be crushed on the sodden ground. The room, too, where Elissa had slept ...

Rowan slipped into bed. She must have dropped off,

otherwise the impact would not have taken her by such surprise, she would have heard the leading up to the secondary cyclone's final outburst, and not leapt up at that sound like a truck discharging a load of metal, like a monstrous wave breaking against a rock. As it was she just ran as she was, still in a pair of Jonathan's pyjamas that Nancy had said would be all right if she tucked up the legs and turned in the sleeves.

In the passage, Jonathan caught her, held her. 'I thought you would be alarmed, little one. There's nothing to fear, it's the last fling.' Without another word, he lifted her bodily and carried her to the lounge, put her in the chair by the still red fire. 'It's over now,' he assured her.

'I . . . I was asleep,' she apologized. 'I woke up and I was scared. I'm sorry, Jonathan, I'm afraid I'll never make a countrywoman.'

'You'll make one,' he said evenly, and she saw he was rolling a cigarette, 'even if I have to belt it into you for the rest of your life.'

'Which,' she flashed, '*you* would do.'

'Which,' he altered blandly, 'I intend to do.'

'Jonathan . . .' she stammered.

'I'm going to make a countrywoman out of you, a tall state countrywoman. You're going to be a Queenslander, Rowan.'

'I won't mind that.'

'But will you mind being – my variety?' He had not lit the cigarette, but he held it aloft, waiting to. Behind the cigarette and the match, his eyes were narrowed.

'What variety is that?'

He said, quite casually, 'A ginger wife.'

'A— What do you mean?'

'I mean that I'm asking you in my own peculiar way to become Mrs. Saxby.'

'Mrs. Jonathan Saxby?'

'There's no other Saxbys around here. Yes. I mean that.' He lit the cigarette, but did not take his eyes from her.

'I don't understand . . . I mean why? . . . why? Why all at once?'

'All at once?' He took the cigarette from his mouth and threw it furiously into the fire, even though he had just made it. 'Why? You ask me that? You must have known how I felt right from that first day.'

'Yes . . . furious that I was an inexperienced newchum, that – that I promptly cried.' She was remembering a fat tear plopping into the black tea that he had passed across.

'And you must have peeped through your weeping and seen someone completely hooked for the first time in his life.'

'You had an alien way of showing it.'

'Ginger is an alien crop.'

'But you were hard, sarcastic.'

'I hadn't bargained on someone like you. I had my trustee duty to fulfil, but I hadn't thought it would be at the expense of someone like you.'

'Then you knew the outcome right from the beginning?'

'Of course,' he said angrily, 'anyone did who had read the will. Everyone knew that the café couldn't keep up its figures when it had to share the trade. If Tom had had legal advice and not written it out himself all this would never have happened.' He paused, 'And I would never have got you.'

'Wait,' Rowan said. At a look in his face she added, 'There are things I must know.'

'The first will be why did I deceive you,' he said wearily. 'I didn't, really, I thought you would have had the elementary sense to have read your uncle's will, to have known that I was included with the others.'

'I hadn't read it, and when you knew I hadn't, why didn't you tell me?'

'Obvious, isn't it, when I knew your obvious reaction.'

'You mean I would have thought you were fighting me at the same time as my step-cousins were fighting me, only in a sneakier way? Yes, I did think that.'

'So,' he said, 'I said nothing.'

'How did Uncle Tom come to adopt you? Was he married? If you were an orphan why do you speak of your parents and grandparents at Narganoo? And who are the Rays?'

'Finished?' he asked. 'Then let me say a word or two. Tom adopted me because he was so damn sorry for me. That's all I can say. All this coast was damn sorry for me. I was damn sorry myself for that kid out there.'

'You?'

'Yes.'

'Out where?'

'Out there on the island. Remember that day I took you?'

'Yes.'

'I grew up there. I had a father. I won't say he was no good, but I won't say he was good, either. Do you recall our beachcomber talk?'

She nodded.

'That was him. Part artist, part sculptor, part writer, part dreamer, part . . . and the most part . . . loafer. I had a mother, but she gave up before I can even remember her, so he must have been hopeless, for a woman has to suffer a lot to leave a child.'

'Poor Jonathan!' She made a little move, but he stopped her.

'No, let me finish first.

'He did a lot of things I want to forget . . . but the final one was to forget me and go away.'

'He left you there!' she said aghast.

'I survived,' he half-grinned, 'and it really was a turning point. Half a dozen of the Tall Staters applied to adopt me. The Narganoo ginger planters, the Rays, childless and wonderful people, officially got me. Your uncle Tom never married, so he couldn't be considered, but if you had known your uncle Tom you would have known, too, that legal niceties meant nothing to him, to Tom I was really his adopted son. He even wrote it in his will.'

'My mother,' said Rowan, 'wrote it in her Bible.'

'Which you sent for. I could have shaken you!'

'Yes, you're good at shaking.'

'Keep it in mind,' he advised, 'because I'm getting mighty sick of all these explanations.'

But there were still breaks in the story, still things she must know.

'You would have ruled against me?' she asked.

'Yes.'

'And benefited yourself?'

He did not answer.

'Jonathan,' she said, 'I have to know. I mean there was mention of a previous will. Did you' . . . she paused . . . 'manipulate that as well?'

'Yes.' He looked at her coolly. 'I did. I made Tom alter it. I would have made him alter this one, I mean as regarded my name, had I known.'

'And whom did that first will benefit?'

Another pause, then: 'Me. I was the sole inheritor. I saw it, and tore it up. *Now* do you understand?'

She sat silent a long time, a lot of the pieces falling into place.

'Your step-cousins,' Jonathan said, 'were run of the mill, no better, no worse – I really mean, Rowan, they wanted their share like most people would. But they went around it the wrong way, they pestered Tom. When I refused to benefit, he went right to the other extreme and selected you.'

'But if I failed, *you*, too. Yet you say you didn't know?'

'No' . . . angrily . . . 'I didn't know.'

Although the room was warm, he put another log on the fire. After a while the wood began to crackle. Rowan could still hear the rain, but indistinctly.

'Now,' she asked, 'what happens?'

'That,' he answered, 'depends entirely on you.'

'I mean' . . . flushing . . . 'as regards the café.'

'It still depends on you.'

'How can it when I'm ruled right out, I mean I'm ruled out now with the decline in profits.'

'You were, but . . .' He paused. After a moment he went on, 'I haven't told you yet. Cosy Corner wasn't so cosy today, it got a bad doing. Even before I came to get you, it had happened.'

'What had?'

'The opposition. The Outlook. Your step-cousins' effort.'

'It was—'

'It was blown away. It's on the weather side, remember, it overlooks the sea.'

'And Tom Thumb?'

'Absolutely intact.'

'Which means I'm the winner?'

He hesitated. 'In a way.'

'In a way . . . Oh, you mean I won't feel good about it? No, Jonathan, I won't. I'm sorry for them.'

'I'm glad to hear you say that. Now we can go on from there.'

'You mean recompense them?'

'Yes. After all, Rowan, they were entitled much more than you were really, entirely more than I.'

'And with the new motorway meeting up at our junction I can do it handsomely, can't I?' Rowan beamed.

'Well . . .' Jonathan evaded.

She looked at him and waited, aware that there was more to come.

'Well, the best laid plans,' he shrugged. 'It happens all the time.'

'What happens?'

'Changes in policy. A new board has taken over and that plan, the one favouring Eats, has been dumped.' He leaned down and picked up a small log, took out a pen-knife and carved a few rough lines on it. 'That's our motorway. That was the proposed junction of the new one.' He scored it through, and scraped another. 'This is the actual one that will come.'

'Missing us?'

'Yes.'

'So . . . no fortune?'

'No.'

'In fact nothing?'

'Nothing,' he said.

'Then how do I recompense my step-cousins?'

'I do.' He was looking at her tentatively. 'I'm a rich man, Rowan. When the Rays took me I got wordly wealth as well as a wealth of love. You'll have to let me do this, pass on some of that double inheritance. Treble, when I count old Tom. Please, my darling.'

My darling. She felt around that. Tasted it. Longed for it.

But still she waited.

'We'll give them all they've expended, and more. They'll have to admit we've been fair. Then Barney and Nancy will go in.'

'In a café where no one stops?'

'Don't you believe it, there'll be callers. Not a gold-mine, but Barney would have hated that, anyway. All he ever wanted was a place by the roadside with the woman he loves. He'll ask her when he's got it, he'll say—'

Rowan broke in: ' "I'll be needing someone permanent in the caff, Nance, how about it?" '

They both laughed.

'But will he accept charity?'

'It won't be. When he knows about the collapse in plans, he'll accept the cheap price we ask. Oh, yes, we'll have to ask something, I know that stubborn cuss.'

Questions were running out. The breaks were nearly all filled. Yet not quite filled.

'You changed your mind about propriety very conveniently when Elissa spent the night here.'

'There was Nancy.'

'I really meant you changed your mind about me.'

'And Nicholas? Elissa told me, and sisters know, that there was nothing there.'

'There could have been,' said Rowan, a little piqued.

'Don't I know it? Haven't I lain awake every night knowing it? But I won't lie awake again, because Nicholas has another love.'

As she looked at him wonderingly, he said, 'Born in the middle of the onslaught . . . by the way, the stud fared well, a sheltered pocket there.'

'Miss Mary?'

'Yes. A fine little filly to be called Miss Mary Too. Nicholas was in his seventh heaven, Rowan, he was absolutely transported. I'm afraid, my darling' . . . my darling again! . . . 'you never came into it.'

'No,' she said softly, and she was seeing Nicholas with his firstborn, his pleasure even greater than Miss Mary's. She saw the little wet, wide-eyed girl being gently handled by that kind, loving man.

'Dear Nicholas,' she said.

She glanced up and found Jonathan's eyes on her, warm, direct. 'I've called you "my darling" twice,' he reproached, 'but all you say is "dear Nicholas".' He waited and still looked at her.

'There is one more thing,' she faltered.

'Yes?'

'Did ... did you give Elissa a ginger flower with her breakfast as well?'

'Elissa? Good lord, no!'

'You gave them to me.'

'... to tell you,' he said.

'Tell me?'

'Down in the Antarctic when a penguin courts he brings a little pebble. Well' ... boyishly ... 'I brought a red ginger flower.'

'To tell me?'

'Yes.'

'Oh, for heaven's sake, Jonathan, tell me *what*?' she demanded. – Oh, what a man!

He got up, crossed to her, picked her up ... still in his tucked-up, turned-in pyjamas.

He said:

'This.'

Why the smile?

... because she has just received her **Free Harlequin Romance Catalogue!**

... and now she has a complete listing of the many, many Harlequin Romances still available.

... and now she can pick out titles by her favorite authors or fill in missing numbers for her library.

You too may have a **Free Harlequin Romance Catalogue** (and a smile!), simply by mailing in the coupon below.

GOLDEN HARLEQUIN LIBRARY

A Treasury of Harlequin Romances!

Many of the all time favorite Harlequin Romance Novels have not been available, until now, since the original printing. But on this special introductory offer, they are yours in an exquisitely bound, rich gold hardcover with royal blue imprint. Three complete unabridged novels in each volume. And the cost is so very low you'll be amazed!

Golden Harlequin Library

Handsome, Hardcover Library Editions at Paperback Prices! ONLY $1.75 each volume.

This very special collection of 30 volumes (there'll be more!) of classic Harlequin Romances would be a distinctive addition to your library. And imagine what a delightful gift they'd make for any Harlequin reader!

Start your collection now. See reverse of this page for full details.

L